Climbing the Stairs

Padma Venkatraman

G. P. Putnam's Sons

This book is dedicated to A. N. Aiyar (my *thatha*)
and Ambujam Venkatraman (my *amma*).

G. P. PUTNAM'S SONS
A division of Penguin Young Readers Group.
Published by The Penguin Group.
Penguin Group (USA) Inc., 375 Hudson Street, New York, NY 10014, U.S.A. Penguin Group
(Canada), 90 Eglinton Avenue East, Suite 700, Toronto, Ontario M4P 2Y3, Canada (a division
of Pearson Penguin Canada Inc.). Penguin Books Ltd, 80 Strand, London WC2R 0RL, England.
Penguin Ireland, 25 St. Stephen's Green, Dublin 2, Ireland (a division of Penguin Books Ltd.).
Penguin Group (Australia), 250 Camberwell Road, Camberwell, Victoria 3124, Australia (a
division of Pearson Australia Group Pty Ltd). Penguin Books India Pvt Ltd, 11 Community
Centre, Panchsheel Park, New Delhi - 110 017, India. Penguin Group (NZ), 67 Apollo Drive,
Rosedale, North Shore 0632, New Zealand (a division of Pearson New Zealand Ltd.). Penguin
Books (South Africa) (Pty) Ltd, 24 Sturdee Avenue, Rosebank, Johannesburg 2196, South Africa.
Penguin Books Ltd, Registered Offices: 80 Strand, London WC2R 0RL, England.

Design by Richard Amari.
Text set in Garamond.

Library of Congress Cataloging-in-Publication Data
Venkatraman, Padma. Climbing the stairs / Padma Venkatraman. p. cm. Summary: In India, in
1941, when her father becomes brain-damaged in a non-violent protest march, fifteen-year-old
Vidya and her family are forced to move in with her father's extended family and become
accustomed to a totally different way of life. [1. Family life—India—Fiction. 2. Prejudices—
Fiction. 3. Brain damage—Fiction. 4. India—History—British occupation, 1790–1947—
Fiction.] I. Title. PZ7.V5578Cl 2008   [Fic]—dc22   2007021757

ISBN 978-0-399-24746-0
1 3 5 7 9 10 8 6 4 2

ACKNOWLEDGMENTS

Thanks to Ms. Viji Varghese for proofreading early drafts; the library staff at the College of William and Mary, Johns Hopkins University, the University of Rhode Island, Lancaster University, Yorktown, Jamestown, and North Kingstown; the editorial team at Penguin for insightful comments; and Rainer Lohmann, Barbara Markowitz, and John Rudolph, for their steadfast support and encouragement.

Contents

Climbing
the
Stairs

August 1941

I still remember the day we celebrated Krishna Jayanthi, the festival of Lord Krishna's birth, at our home in Bombay. The drive was drenched with the juice of fallen *jamun* fruit and the sand of Mahim beach gleamed like a golden plate in the afternoon sunlight. Whispers of heat rose from the tar road and shivered toward the slumbering Arabian Sea.

I had folded up my ankle-length skirt and was getting ready to climb up the jamun tree. A warm breeze blew around my bare knees. My brother's brown legs were already wrapped around the roughness of the main trunk, clinging on like a monkey to its mother's body. Kitta was eighteen and he'd just started college, but though his voice had recently deepened and the first fuzzy promise of a black mustache shadowed his upper lip, he still looked more a boy than a man. Our dog, Raja, was yapping loudly on the ground, wagging his tail.

I spread an old rug on the ground beneath the tree and climbed up after him, scraping my skin against its lumpy bark. Soon we were shaking the branches, watching the ripe purple fruit rain onto the rug like a monsoon shower.

"Vidya!" amma called. I glanced down. I could see her disapproving gaze from where she stood, barefoot on our verandah, the open patio in front of our home. Ever since I had turned fifteen and started wearing a half sari, she had been hoping that I would become womanly, not climb any more trees, run no more races across the beach sands and stop playing volleyball at Walsingham Girls' School (she felt it wasn't ladylike).

She held a bowl and a small white rag in her hands. "Would you like to decorate the verandah?"

Every year we would paint tiny white footprints all the way across the red cement on the front steps and verandah, into the marble-flecked mosaic floor of the house, through the great hall and to the prayer room in the back; footsteps to lead Lord Krishna into our home. I didn't mind. It was one of the few girlish tasks I enjoyed.

"I'm going to paint some Krishna feet," I told Kitta. I climbed down and patted Raja on his head. I tried to rinse the purple stains off my hands at the brass tap in the corner of the garden, scrubbing my hands with the hairy hide of a fallen coconut. I straightened out my skirt and walked up the stairs.

"Thank you," amma said, forcing the corners of her mouth upward. Her smiles had been different ever since appa had started coming home late. The bright white sign still hung on the door of the clinic behind our home, slightly askew, stating in English, Hindi and Marathi that the doctor worked from nine o'clock to five o'clock during the week and from nine until twelve on Saturdays. But he no longer kept those hours. He went missing, at least a few days each week, returning after Kitta and I were back from school. Some evenings, amma sent us to bed before we saw him.

"Where do you go, appa?" I had asked, and he had patted my head and replied that he had started another job.

"What job?" I had asked. "Why do you need two jobs?"

To which he had simply replied, "Nothing for you to worry about."

The only time I enjoyed hearing him say those words was when he had said them to amma, a month ago, on her birthday.

He had taken us to Mr. Sultan's jewelry store. Kitta and I had been sitting on plush satin-backed chairs in the showroom, clinking the ice cubes in the tall glasses of sweet lime juice that the store hand had brought to us on a silver tray, trying to see which of us could swirl the liquid faster without spilling it.

"Everything looks beautiful on you," appa told amma. Pairs of gold earrings were set out on the glass case in front of them, glimmering against the blue velvet that lined their boxes. Amma held up a diamond-studded flower design beside her perfect crescent-shaped earlobe, then gasped when Mr. Sultan mentioned the price and put it back.

"Get it," appa said, smiling indulgently.

"But it's so expensive," amma said worriedly. "Can we really afford it? Shouldn't we be saving for Vidya's dowry?"

Appa had taken one look at the shock on my face and said to her, "Nothing for you to worry about yet."

My marital status hadn't been mentioned again, but surely it was only a matter of time. Every other fifteen-year-old in the fifth form of Walsingham Girls' School had had her horoscope sent off to families with eligible sons. I was determined to delay its distribution. That horror of a document was only a page long, but it was filled with rectangles that told the position of the planets on the day of one's birth, and before any marriage was arranged, a soothsayer had to look at the horoscopes of the girl and the boy to make sure they were compatible.

Would my parents let me go to college after I finished sixth form? I wondered about that for the umpteenth time. Amma was so happy being a housewife that she was convinced I needed to get "settled" and married off to a "nice" boy from a "good" family, sooner rather than later. I couldn't think how to explain to her that I wanted more. Anyway, appa made all the big decisions.

"What's the frown for?" Kitta yelled, interrupting my memories as he peered down at me through the tree branches.

"Nothing," I said. Today wasn't a day for worrying about marriage. It was the festival of Krishna Jayanthi.

I dipped my hands into the cool, white, watery rice paste,

wetting a corner of the small square cloth with it, and then I squeezed the paste out of the rag, carefully drawing tiny footsteps with circles for each toe. I loved the story of mischievous Krishna, an incarnation of God, born on the seventh day of the seventh month of Shravan, with skin the blue-black of a midnight sky. Krishna's sermons were embedded in the *Bhagavad Gita,* but although he could be serious when he was fighting evil, he was also playful and he never lost his sense of humor.

The roar of our car interrupted my thoughts. The wrought-iron gate creaked as Xavier, our watchman, pushed it shut and retired to his room at the foot of the drive. Appa was in the backseat of the blue Austin. I waved at him, raising my right hand, which held the soaked rag. Blobs of rice paste spattered across the floor.

Appa didn't smile or wave back, as he usually did. He threw open the door when the car stopped without waiting for Suruve, our driver, to hold it open for him. Raja raced up to him, barking a joyous welcome, but appa didn't stop to stroke him.

Amma reappeared on the verandah. She had tucked a string of *kanakambaram* flowers in her hair, and they peeped above her head in an orange halo that matched the heavy, gold-embroidered silk sari into which she had changed. Her plump cheeks were dimpled in a welcoming smile, but she was not gazing at appa. Instead, her eyes were fixed on appa's *kurtha.*

Or rather, on the strange rust-colored stain spread across his loose, collarless shirt.

"I'm all right," he told her. "It's not mine. I'm fine. Really."

What wasn't his? I wondered, staring.

He seemed not to see me and walked up to amma, putting his strong, muscular arm across her shoulders in a rare display of affection. He ran a finger across her forehead, ironing out the worried creases. His broad-shouldered frame filled the doorway.

Amma looked small and vulnerable when she stood next to him. She darted a frightened look at me, as though to warn him not to say too much. Then she straightened up against him, saying, "Shall we have some tea?"

"Yes, and I should change before that." He let her go and smiled down at me at last. "What beautiful footprints, Vidya!"

I grinned up at him proudly. "Appa, I was thinking of what we could do for the weekend. Rifka says there's a new cinema theater that's opened up, and she says it's not all reserved for whites, and there's a section on the ground floor where Indians are allowed—"

Appa pinched my cheek affectionately. I expected him to say yes, as he usually did, but instead he said, "Sorry, but we can't go out this weekend. Your eldest uncle is coming over on Saturday morning, and we need to spend time with him."

I didn't try to hide my disappointment. "Periappa's visiting? Why?"

"He was up north on a business trip, so he's decided to stop and see us before returning to Madras."

I scowled.

"None of that, young lady." Appa wagged a warning finger at me. "You're old enough to stop acting childish. He's my elder brother, and you'll respect him." Before he stepped indoors, he added, "And remember to tie Raja up Saturday morning before he comes. You know how periappa feels about dogs."

After he left, I stared glumly at the floor.

Kitta descended from his perch and walked toward me. "Come on," he said, grinning. "It's not that bad, is it?"

"I guess not," I conceded. "It's just—I can't believe he's appa's brother, can you? He's so, so—"

"Orthodox?" Kitta suggested.

"Yes," I agreed. "Appa doesn't care that we're Brahmin, but periappa never forgets it, does he? He treats our servants like dirt just because they're a lower caste."

"Most Brahmins like throwing their weight around," Kitta said.

"That's not what we're supposed to do, is it?" I said. "We're supposed to read the scriptures and teach and pray. Live an ascetic lifestyle." According to appa, caste was a social evil, not a Hindu belief. He said caste had begun with a relatively compassionate idea of a code of conduct: that the Brahmins, who were scholars and priests, should never take up arms or seek wealth or power. Caste wasn't meant to be hereditary or exclusive or hierarchical, but Brahmins and other "high" castes now oppressed those without education or wealth.

Kitta looked thoughtful. "Most people are like periappa," he said. "Not that I'm trying to excuse him or anything. It's not easy to be different, the way appa is. It is odd they're brothers, though," Kitta mused.

I gave him a cheeky grin. "Actually, it isn't strange at all," I said. "I know why they're so different. Periappa can't really help it. He's the older one, and as we all know, the second kid always gets the brains."

Kitta laughed. "Okay. You won that round."

I glowed, feeling pleased with myself. Kitta was far wittier than I was. It wasn't often that he couldn't think of a come-back.

"Here's something that'll make you feel even better," Kitta continued. "Periappa isn't bringing periamma and Malati along."

I smiled, relieved that my aunt and cousin weren't coming. Most of our cousins were male and much older than we were, but periappa had a daughter, Malati, who was a year older than I was and as unlike me as her father was from mine. She liked cooking and sewing and staying indoors to gossip with older women. "That really is something to be thankful for," I said, cheering up again. "How long is he staying, do you know?"

"Periappa arrives Saturday and leaves Sunday morning. Short trip," Kitta said.

"How come you know all that and I don't know a thing?" I asked. "How come they always tell *you* every detail?"

"Because I'm older and smarter," he said, smirking.

I soaked the rag in rice paste and threw it at him. He caught it deftly, wiping off the white spot that landed on his nose. "You're going to smear the verandah with white drops instead of drawing a nice neat line of footprints."

"Why don't you help me if you're that concerned about how our verandah looks?" I asked.

"I will, actually." He got up and headed toward the house.

Kitta should have been the girl in our family, I thought as he disappeared inside to fetch another rag. Kitta was always ready to help, he was hard to annoy, he rarely argued with anyone and he could see the bright side of any situation. Returning to the verandah, he crouched and started scraping off the mess I had made.

Kitta and I worked quietly for a while side by side. My eyes fell on the *kolam*, the geometric pattern that our maid, Ponni, drew on the front steps every morning with rice flour. Today, in honor of the festival, she had made an elaborate swastika design.

"Why do the Nazis wear our swastikas?" I wondered out loud. "I thought they didn't like colored people."

"No idea why they took our religious symbol," he said, following my gaze and staring at the kolam. "It doesn't make sense."

I thought of the war. The British were fighting with three countries they called the Axis: Germany, Italy and Japan. Indians, technically subjects of the British crown, ought to have been on the side of the British. But I wasn't certain if we were or not because Indians were busy struggling for freedom from British rule. Gandhiji, leader of the Indian National Congress Party, said we had to throw the British out without using violence. But it wasn't clear what he or our other leaders felt about the British war with the Axis.

"Kitta," I said, "how come Gandhiji and the rest say we're against Hitler but then tell us not to enlist in the British Indian Army? If we disagree with Hitler, then shouldn't we be fighting him?"

Kitta knitted his brows thoughtfully. "It's a good question. I wonder about it a lot."

"So what do you think?"

"I think it's tough. We don't like Hitler because he says his race is superior. But the British think they're better than us, so we don't like them either."

"Because the British think we can't rule ourselves, you mean?" I asked. "Because they keep us out of first-class compartments in trains and that sort of thing?"

"Exactly. The British think we're uncivilized because we're darker than they are. Hitler wants to rule over anybody and everybody, white, black and everything in between. So what's the difference?" Kitta paused. "Plus the British didn't even bother to ask Gandhiji's opinion about the war. They just went off and ordered Indians to fight, like we're their slaves or something."

"So why did we take part in that other big war, Kitta, the one the British and everyone fought in 1914 or whenever, when appa was young? How come we didn't sit that one out?"

"The British promised us freedom if we helped them then," Kitta said.

"They broke their word?"

"Looks like they cheated us, doesn't it?" Kitta said. "Here we are, still a colony, with whites-only signs all over the place."

I was silent. Appa always said Gandhiji was a great soul. That Indians were a peaceful people, that killing and wars went against our tradition of nonviolence, of *ahimsa*. We listened to news on the radio every night, and I knew what appa felt about our freedom struggle, but he never voiced opinions about the faraway war.

My thoughts turned to appa's disheveled appearance. "Kitta, did you see the stain on appa's kurtha?"

A pause.

"Did you, Kitta?"

"No," he said unconvincingly.

I sat back on my haunches and looked at him. He was kneeling, scraping hard at a spot that looked quite clean.

"Something's going on that everyone knows about except me," I said.

"Rubbish."

"Then look me in the eye and tell me you don't know where appa was." I had always been able to outstare Kitta.

"I don't know where appa goes," he said. His eyes caught my fierce gaze fleetingly.

"But you have an idea, don't you?"

"Maybe," he mumbled.

Amma chose that moment to interrupt us. "You've done a lovely job, Vidya. I've painted the footsteps indoors, so we're finished. Why don't you go in and change into a sari before we meet in the *poojai* room?"

"Don't you want the jamun fruit we collected?" I said, trying to procrastinate. I did want to see how amma had decorated our prayer room for the festive occasion, but more than anything, I wanted to find out how much Kitta knew about appa.

"I'll ask Ponni to collect the fruit. Now be a good girl, *kanna*, and get changed."

I sighed. Amma was calling me *kanna* again, a term of endearment usually reserved for a little child.

Kitta sighed too, with relief that he had been able to wriggle out of my questioning.

Krishna Jayanthi

I went indoors, had a quick wash and carefully reapplied a red *pottu* in the center of my forehead, looking into the tiny mirror to make sure I drew the dot in the correct spot. Then I pulled out a maroon sari, buttoned my puff-sleeved blouse, slipped on my petticoat and called our maid, Ponni, to help me arrange the sari's pleats.

"You look nice," Ponni said approvingly. I pursed my lips as I made my way into the sitting room, taking the mincing steps that my sari permitted. Half saris didn't hamper me as much, but in a few years' time I'd be too old to wrap myself in anything but a full six yards of cloth. I needed to practice.

Kitta saw me almost trip over the sari's flowing folds, and he choked over the cup of *chai* he was sipping. I stuck my tongue out at him. Amma didn't notice, and she smiled approvingly at my effort, though still tight-lipped. I smiled back at her, wondering why she wasn't as radiant as usual. Was she worried about periappa's visit too? When he visited, it was a lot harder on her than on the rest of us. She had to wait on periappa hand and foot.

Appa was breathing in the chai's mingled scent of freshly crushed cardamom and strong black tea. I pulled up a wicker chair and sat down next to him.

"Appa, where were you? Why aren't you at the clinic every day?" I asked.

Amma shook her head, as though to tell appa to stay silent.

"Tell me?" I wheedled. "Please? I'm old enough to know. Does Kitta know?"

Appa looked worn-out. He took a sip of the sweet, milky tea from his steaming cup. "I'm doing some new things. Volunteer work."

"Volunteer work?" I asked. "Why?"

"I suppose you could say it makes me feel fulfilled," he said.

"Don't we keep you feeling fulfilled?" I asked, hoping to coax him into saying more.

He smiled but didn't answer. "So what did you do in school today, Vidya?"

I didn't want to change the topic, but I couldn't help chattering about school and volleyball and my best friend, Rifka. Rifka was Jewish, but other than that, she was like my twin sister. We were the same height, our hair was the same shade of black, we played the same sports, we laughed at the same things and we had even got our first period the same day, nearly a year ago. Kitta teased her as much as he teased me when she came over, and I bossed over her little brother just as much as she did.

By the time I got through telling appa about my day, it was prayer time and Ponni was clearing away the remains of our tea.

We gathered around the household altar in the poojai room, and amma's voice rose in a Sanskrit chant. She poured oil into the old brass lamp and lit the wick. When the small flame began to dance, she placed a camphor cube on her handheld lamp and lit it with the flame. Pungent smoke curled into the air from the burning camphor and twirled together with the brown tendrils that were rising from the glowing incense sticks.

I looked at the brightly colored picture of the blue God Krishna, the bronze image of Nataraja, lord of dance, and the sandalwood figurines of Lakshmi, the goddess of wealth, and Saraswathi, the goddess of learning. Amma offered the blessed food, the small plate with fruit, milk, curds and sweets, to each of us, beginning with me. The ritual was comforting, and by the time it was over, the spicy fragrance of the special Krishna Jayanthi feast wafted in from the kitchen and drove the worries about appa out of my mind.

We didn't talk much at dinner, enjoying the wonderful meal

in silence. "You make the best dishes in the whole world," I told amma after I finished.

"The cook did most of it," she said. "I just sprinkled the spices on at the very end." But I could tell she was pleased. Unlike me, she enjoyed being the chef.

After Ponni cleared the dishes, we sat together in the main hall. The Murphy radio crackled to life as appa twiddled the black knob, searching through the static for a spot where the sound was clearest. A crisp British accent entered the room. There wasn't much news about the Indian freedom struggle. Instead, the voice droned on about the British prime minister, Churchill, meeting the president of America, Roosevelt. Apparently they had quite a good chat, and America agreed to help Britain and not the Nazis. But if it had been Churchill's mission to get American troops to fight alongside his own, it sounded as though he had failed. The news broadcast ended with the sound of Big Ben, the huge London clock, sounding out the hour.

Appa turned the Murphy off, and I yawned. Tomorrow was Friday, and I had to wake up early to be at school on time. But there was something I still needed to know before I went to bed.

"Appa, you're keeping secrets from me," I said.

"What secret do you think I am keeping?" he asked.

Amma frowned.

"Where do you go these days?" I asked appa. "What's your new volunteer work all about?"

Appa looked at me thoughtfully for a while and then said slowly, "You have a right to know. I'm helping our freedom fighters. I attend some of the nonviolent protests."

"Oh," I said, taken aback that he'd confessed.

Amma's mouth was set in a thin line. I didn't see what she was so unhappy about. She ought to be proud. My father was taking part in our freedom struggle!

"So how come you told Kitta and not me?" I asked.

"Kitta only knows because he asked before you did," appa said. "Don't think you can press charges against me for differential treatment."

"See," Kitta said smugly. "I asked first. Always ahead of you, that's me."

"None of that," appa said to him firmly before I could think of a withering retort. "Now, shall we retire? Bedtime, I think."

I agreed, partly because I couldn't think of how to tell appa that I admired him without it sounding silly.

I lay in bed, the excitement keeping me awake. At school tomorrow, I'd tell Rifka what a hero my father was. She could be trusted with that secret for sure.

Amma came into my room to turn out the light, looking more withdrawn than usual.

"Amma," I said. "Why do you look so worried?"

"Do I look worried?" she asked evasively.

"Yes," I said. Maybe she had a lot left to do before periappa's visit. "I'll help you as soon as I get back from school tomorrow," I offered. "I know you have to send the cook away and prepare all the meals yourself because periappa won't eat anything that isn't cooked by Brahmin hands."

Amma's cheeks dimpled as she smiled. "Thank you, kanna. That's sweet of you," she said. "But you should finish your homework after school so you'll be free the rest of the weekend. I'll manage fine on my own. Periappa is only staying for a day." Before I could ask anything else, she wished me good night and turned out the light.

I sat up in bed, thoughts buzzing in my head like a mosquito. When I finally drifted off into a disturbed sleep, I dreamed that the red-brown stain on my father's kurtha kept growing bigger and brighter.

Rifka

At school the next day, I couldn't wait to tell Rifka all about appa. She came in late, after the morning assembly. I tried slipping her a note during our first lesson, but our teacher, Mrs. Batlivala, saw me scribbling and walked over to take a look.

"What are you up to, Vidya?" she asked.

"Sorry, ma'am," I said.

She glanced at the note but didn't ask me to hand it over. She was the nicest teacher at school, and I felt guilty that I hadn't been paying attention.

"Ma'am, I won't do it again," I said earnestly.

She let me off easily, as always. I tried hard to pay attention to her for the rest of the morning, but I couldn't wait for the lunch bell to ring.

Rifka and I found our favorite lunch spot—a concrete bench under the neem tree. I brushed off a fallen neem seed, sat beside her and pried open my *tiffin* box to see what I had for lunch: rice and lentils in the first compartment of the lunch box, curd rice in the second and four *seedais* in the third. Amma knew Rifka loved the sesame balls, and she must have put a few aside after yesterday's feast.

I handed Rifka a seedai. "My favorite," she said, crunching into it happily. "Are you doing anything special this weekend?"

I shook my head and sucked gently on the candied sesame seeds in my mouth.

"Do you want to come home with me on Saturday?" she asked. "You haven't been over for a while."

"I can't," I said, rolling my eyes. "Periappa is visiting."

"Your eldest uncle?" she asked sympathetically.

"Yes, that one."

Rifka knew all about periappa. Every summer, we asked the old couple who lived in the flat that occupied the entire top floor of our two-story building to look after Raja. Our servants left for their annual holidays. Then we took the one-and-a-half-day train ride to Madras, the coastal city where my father's family lived, because my father felt duty bound to visit them for at least a few weeks each year.

My grandfather was fairly wealthy, but he lived the way Indians had lived for generations—under the same roof as his married sons. That was the tradition: the extended family stayed together. I didn't get more than a glimpse of Kitta or appa in the summers because the men lived upstairs and the women lived downstairs in that house. There was just one room reserved for husbands and wives to sleep together, and the couples took turns spending nights in it. The only good thing about going to Madras every summer was that as soon as school started again, I could make Rifka laugh by telling her funny stories about appa's family.

"At least we don't have to live with periappa all year," I said, and tried to bring the conversation around to my father. "Thank goodness my father came to Bombay. That's a blessing."

"Your father is so nice," Rifka said.

I smiled. "He is," I agreed. "So can you keep a secret about him? A really big secret?"

Rifka's dark eyes widened at once. She loved secrets.

"You can't tell a soul," I said seriously. "Not your mother, not your father, not your little brother. No one."

"I promise," she said. I knew I could trust her.

"This is really, really big," I said, my voice dropping to a whisper.

"Okay," she whispered back.

I took a quick look around us. The yard was empty. "My dad's a freedom fighter," I said.

"A freedom fighter?" she gasped, gazing at me in awe. "Really?"

"Would I lie about a thing like that?"

"That's fantastic," she breathed. "Did he just join the

freedom movement? What does he do? How long have you known?"

"I just found out yesterday," I told her. "He's been away a lot these past weeks, so I pestered him a little about what he was up to, and he told me. I don't know exactly where he goes or anything, but I'll tell you if I find out."

"My best friend is the daughter of a freedom fighter," Rifka said in a thrilled whisper. "I can't believe it!"

Her reaction had been every bit as satisfying as I'd hoped. "I have the best—" I was about to say I had the best family ever, but I caught myself in time. My family was very unusual, and I knew it, but she had a wonderful family too. "I have the best friend ever," I finished, and we smiled at each other.

The bell rang all too quickly, forcing us to return to class. Now Rifka was too excited to concentrate on the lesson. She knew she couldn't ask questions about appa in the classroom, where anyone might overhear what she said, but she chattered on and on about all sorts of other things.

Mrs. Batlivala caught us whispering. "Girls, girls," she said, wagging her head at us. She made me get up and move all the way to the other end of the classroom. We were forced to sit apart for the rest of the afternoon.

When the bell rang at the day's end and we walked out of the building, Rifka linked hands with me and asked conspiratorially, "Can I come over and see your father sometime next week?"

"You've met him loads of times," I pointed out.

"Yes, but that was before I knew he was a hero," she said.

I laughed. "We'll have you over after periappa leaves," I promised. "Sometime early next week."

Rifka looked thrilled.

I saw our Austin stop in front of the school gates. Kitta was inside, his nose buried in a book. Suruve held the door open for me. I slid into the backseat and glanced out the rear window. Rifka was still beaming at me joyfully. We waved madly at each other until the Austin turned a bend in the road and she was out of sight.

Mahim Beach

I leaped out of the car and raced Kitta up the front steps. Kitta finished ahead of me, as he always did. Raja bounded toward us, jumped up and licked my face.

"Down, Raja, down," I said to him, not very firmly. I removed my shoes and stuck them in the rack outside the front door before entering the house. Appa looked up from his newspaper as I walked in. I was surprised and pleased to see that he was home early.

"How was school today?" he asked.

"Wonderful," I told him.

"Good," he said, returning to his paper. I went to my room and changed out of my school uniform. I pulled my homework notebooks out, then went to the dining table.

"Need any help?" appa asked briefly.

"Thanks, but no," I said. "Mrs. Batlivala didn't give us much to do. Can we go for a walk today after I finish?"

"Of course," he said, starting to scan the paper again.

By the time I was done, amma and Kitta were ready for a

walk too. Ponni had left for the weekend already. Amma and appa always sent the servants away when periappa came. My parents were embarrassed by the way he treated them. At the extended family home where periappa lived, there were four servants—a cook, two maids and an old gardener—but they were treated very differently from our domestic staff. The only servant allowed into the kitchen and the dining room was the old Brahmin widow who helped to cook, but even she wasn't allowed to handle curds or milk. The other three servants were not Brahmin and because of their inferior caste, they weren't allowed to enter the dining room and the kitchen.

"What are you thinking about?" appa asked as we stepped out of the house together.

"Nothing," I said. I tethered Raja to his leash, and we walked together along the sea face. The cool evening breeze ruffled my hair. Waves crawled lazily up the beach. The scent of roasted groundnuts wafted in our direction from a stall a few feet ahead.

"Appa, may we have some roasted nuts?" I asked.

"Of course," he said indulgently. Then he added, "If your mother doesn't mind, that is."

"Street food could give them jaundice or typhoid," amma said.

"I'm sure it's safe," appa said to her. "The children have eaten here before. The nuts are roasted anyway and in their shells."

Kitta grinned at me. Appa and amma always went through that routine.

"Don't get too much," amma said as appa walked up to the groundnut stall. "Or else they won't be hungry for dinner tonight."

"Amma, we always save space for your meals," I assured her. She smiled. The man made a cone out of newspaper and stuffed it full of groundnuts. Appa handed me one first, then Kitta. The cone was warm and I opened the top carefully.

The pavement ended, and we walked along the sandy beach. It was bustling with people, but we managed to find a fairly secluded spot, and we sat down together.

I stared at Kitta and compared him to appa. Kitta's profile was startlingly like appa's. He was still on the skinny side, but his shoulders were starting to fill out. One day he'd be as muscular and handsome as appa was.

I wondered how I'd look when I was grown. My body had taken on the shape of a woman's, but I was already at least a head taller than amma and I would never look as demure and petite as she did.

I finished the groundnuts and folded the empty cone into a small, neat square. The sun was slipping, red and tired, into the blue bed of the Arabian Sea.

By the time we returned to the house, dusk had fallen over the waters and the first stars were glimmering up above. I loved

Friday evenings. Every Friday, amma did a special poojai before we ate, and after we finished supper, we sat together reading instead of listening to news on the radio.

Ponni was gone, so we all helped clear away the dinner dishes and wash them. Amma rinsed the food off, I scrubbed them with the hide of a coconut until they sparkled and appa and Kitta set them out on the counter to dry.

At reading time, I buried myself in *The Return of Sherlock Holmes,* which Rifka had lent me. Amma leafed through the latest issue of *Anandaviketan* magazine. For a while, the silence was broken only by the rustle of someone turning a page.

When I slapped my book shut and looked up, I noticed with surprise that the cover of Kitta's book had a picture of a soldier. What was it about boys and wars?

Appa's laughter rippled into my thoughts. "Is something the matter?" He chucked me under the chin gently. "Your face is all scrunched up."

"Why do you let Kitta read war books?" I asked. "You talk about nonviolence and here's Kitta, immersing himself in stuff about the glory of war."

Appa looked amused. "So what do you think I should do? Censor his right to read?"

Kitta looked up. The two of them exchanged knowing smiles.

"Of course I don't think you should take away anyone's freedom. Not even Kitta's," I said. "But how come you don't care that he likes wars so much? That's what I want to know."

"It's all quite complex, Vidya," he said. "I don't know if war is always wrong."

"You think war is okay sometimes?" I asked, surprised.

He took a while to answer that. "I believe in ahimsa," he said. "But I don't like saying nonviolence is always right and war is always wrong. After all, I'm a Hindu."

I was startled. "Hindus have right and wrong, don't they?" I asked.

He smiled. He liked discussing Hindu philosophy. "Some of our books speak of *yuga dharma*, the idea that what is right depends on the time, the place and the circumstance."

"But war is about killing people," I objected. "Killing is never right, is it?"

"No, I don't suppose it is," he said slowly. "But then again, I don't believe it's my right to tell anyone else how to think. Not even my own children."

Kitta butted in. "Besides, there's no one set of rules about right and wrong in Hinduism, is there, the way Christians have the Ten Commandments and Muslims have the Koran?"

Appa smiled. "How can we have just one rule book when to us every compassionate spirit is an avatar, an incarnation of the same one God?"

I hadn't thought much about the implications of not having one book and of accepting that our one God could take a million forms. Hinduism did not categorically state what was good and bad; there were no dogmatic rules; instead, the religion gave suggestions on how to act with compassion.

When amma came to my room that night, she quoted a passage from the *Bhagavad Gita,* "In whatever way people approach me, even so do I bless and love them. For many are the paths of worship, and all end in me."

I smiled at her. It was my favorite Hindu prayer because it told me that although Rifka and I called God by different names, we were praying to the same Being. I repeated the prayer to myself, looking at the dark silhouette of the neem tree outside my window, until I fell asleep.

The Chess Game

Sheets of rain poured from the skies on Saturday morning before my uncle's visit. Just as well, I thought. After periappa arrived, I'd be under house arrest all day anyway.

I tried to use the rain as an excuse to keep Raja inside, but amma was firm. "Put him on the back verandah outside your room," she said. "It's dry there."

"Sorry," I said to Raja, who yipped reproachfully as I wound his leash around a pillar. "You're a good dog, but you get punished because of my dad's stupid brother. The minute periappa leaves, I'll set you free. Promise."

I went to Kitta's room and found him sitting straight as a coconut tree, thoughtfully moving the pieces on his chessboard. He loved chess so much he played on his own sometimes. I hated the game—probably because I always lost and he always won. But if I played, it might put him in a good enough mood to answer my questions.

"Shall we play some chess till periappa comes?" I offered.

"You want to play chess?" Kitta raised his eyebrows in surprise. "That's new." He turned the board so the ebony pieces faced me and started lining up his ivory pawns. I pulled up a low stool and arranged my carved wooden pieces on the squares.

"You've got the king and queen in the wrong places," he pointed out, switching them for me.

A few moves into the game, after he took my horse with a gleeful chuckle, I got down to business. "Kitta, how does appa help the protesters?"

"Sometimes they need doctors," he answered. The game had definitely made him lower his guard.

"Why do they need doctors during a nonviolent protest march?"

"Because only *we're* nonviolent. The British are as violent as can be. Haven't you paid attention to the news lately?"

I have, I wanted to say, but I just sort of blocked that part out. "Your move," I said aloud.

"Check," he said in a satisfied tone before going on. "The British beat the protesters, and the protesters don't beat back. That's ahimsa. That's nonviolence, see?"

I did not want to look at the picture that was emerging in my mind. I stared at the black and white chess squares.

"Check," Kitta repeated, looking up at me. "Don't look so worried—you can move your king this way, and you'll be out of danger. Here, look." He moved my king for me.

"Thanks," I muttered softly.

"You're worried about appa, aren't you?" His voice was suddenly gentle. "Look, little sister, that's why I didn't want to tell you yesterday."

"I'm not little."

"Don't worry, then, okay?" He gazed at me with undisguised concern. "It's not like anyone beats up the doctors. When the protestors get beaten, the doctors pick them up and patch them up. They're safe the whole time."

"I'm not worrying," I said. "I know appa is fine." I rested my face in my hands and pretended to immerse myself in the game.

Kitta darted glances at me until he seemed reassured that I was all right.

I wasn't. In my mind's eye, my chess pieces had grown into lines of dark-skinned men marching forward, being beaten by a white army and crumpling one by one into my father's waiting arms, bloodstains blossoming across their shoulders.

"Checkmate," Kitta announced as amma knocked on the door to let us know that periappa had arrived.

Periappa

Kitta and I stood on the verandah together. Appa parked the car and periappa stepped out, a turban covering his straggly hair. He straightened the short coat he wore over his *panchaka-cham,* the traditional lower garment. It was an odd way to dress: the coat was a concession to the British, while the lower garment and the turban were Indian tradition.

Appa picked up periappa's suitcases and strode up the stairs. He looked sleeker and more muscular than ever with his older brother waddling in his wake. Periappa puffed and mopped the sweat from his brow, as though getting up the five steps to the verandah was a huge effort. He came to a stop a few feet away from us, his stomach wobbling. He wiped his fleshy nose on his coat sleeve and then gazed at us with watery eyes. I tried not to stare at the hair sprouting out of his ears or the large mole on his upper lip that looked like a squashed fly.

Kitta prostrated himself before periappa, and amma followed. After the two of them finished, I went through the motions of bowing to periappa so respectfully that amma looked pleasantly surprised. I usually couldn't get through that ritual without a grimace—periappa was one of the last people from whom I wanted a blessing.

I was too preoccupied to respond to periappa's comments at lunch. When periappa said, "Ah, Vidya, you've learned to be silent at last. Maybe we'll find you a husband despite your tanned complexion," I didn't point out that he didn't have to help me get married. Instead, I mixed the rice and golden *rasam* sauce into a sticky paste with my fingers, rolled some of it into a ball and stuck it in my mouth.

My silence made amma so happy that she patted my hand and said to me in a whisper, "You are becoming so well behaved, Vidya." I was glad she couldn't tell I'd finally realized that someone else's dried blood had stained appa's kurtha. I tried to look at her sweetly, as though I really was too grown up to be irritated by periappa.

I sat quietly all through the afternoon. When the adults left to have their siesta, I went to my room, shut the door and thought more about my conversation with Kitta. I had seen policemen with *lathis*—metal-tipped wooden sticks that looked narrow and innocuous. Could they beat hard enough to break someone's skin? I could not imagine what it felt like to be beaten with a lathi stick. No one had ever raised a hand against me.

I said very little even after we sat at the table for the evening meal. I was silent as amma served curry and then ladled steaming brown *sambhar* on the mounds of rice on our silver plates.

"Malati's wedding date has been set," periappa announced. "She was chosen the first time she was seen—no surprise, of course, with her fair skin and mild manners. An excellent match too. Son of Diwan Bahadur A. V. Ramalingam Aiyar. The man who built the Periyar dam."

"Diwan Bahadur?" appa said. "He uses that title still?"

"Of course," periappa said. "Why shouldn't he? He's the chief engineer of the Madras presidency."

"Our leaders asked us to renounce titles granted by the British, not flaunt them," appa said.

"Our leaders ask for all sorts of things," periappa said nonchalantly. "If we did everything they wanted, we wouldn't wear anything but homespun."

Kitta and I exchanged a glance. Appa had given up wearing British-made cloth three years ago to protest the unfair British practice of taking raw cotton from our farmers and selling the woven cloth back to us at outrageous prices. He had given us long lectures about the indigo famines, when the British forced our farmers to grow indigo to dye cloth instead of food to feed their families.

"I get by wearing *khadi*," appa said. I could tell he was putting considerable effort into keeping his voice low. "The British systematically destroyed our industries and crafts. They cut off the hands of our weavers. They raped our wealth. I think the least any Indian can do is boycott foreign goods."

"You live in a cocoon, Venkat," periappa said. "You have your own personal clinic." He glared at appa, his double chin quivering. "The rest of us have to work in this country. We work for the British. If I didn't wear a coat, I wouldn't be allowed to enter my office."

Appa ran the fingers of his left hand through his hair and rested his elbow on the table. "We must show them our pride in our cultural heritage. In some small way, every one of us must."

"You can afford to be idealistic, Venkat," periappa went on. "Most of us don't have that luxury."

The muscles of appa's face twitched, but before he could say anything, periappa continued, "Anyway, the British have given us some good things, you know. Railways and an education system."

"They destroyed our ancient education system and replaced it with one that teaches us that everything Western is good and everything Indian is primitive and bad. Do you believe that? You think they did it to help us somehow?" Appa's voice was shaking and he was almost shouting.

Kitta's eyes twinkled and I grinned. Appa hardly ever told anyone off, least of all his elder brother. It was entertaining to watch.

Periappa stared at appa speechlessly. Before he could find

his voice, amma laid her hand on appa's arm and cut in, "Our heartiest congratulations on arranging the marriage. When is the wedding?"

Appa gave her a somewhat grudging smile.

Periappa seemed relieved that amma had changed the subject. He answered her quickly. "December first to the third, by the English calendar. About ten days after the Karthigai festival." Periappa sucked noisily at the sambhar that was trickling down his fingers. "This sambhar is rather watery, I must say. Next time you are in Madras, you must learn my wife's recipe." He belched and rubbed his belly.

Kitta caught me looking at him. He wrinkled his nose, pretended to belch and rubbed his stomach. I suppressed a giggle.

"You are going to get Malati married before she finishes school?" appa asked.

"Yes, yes," periappa said.

"But—" appa began. I saw amma pluck at the corner of his kurtha. He paused.

"Do tell us more about the groom's family," amma said. "Does he have many brothers and sisters? Where exactly do they live? And what has he studied?"

I lost track of the conversation until it was time to help amma clear away the dishes. Kitta and appa washed their hands and went to the living room to entertain periappa. When we were done, we joined the men in the hall, where they were listening to the radio.

"You let Vidya listen?" periappa said, looking astonished as we sat down with them.

Appa nodded. The reporter was saying something about a blitzkrieg. The Germans were bombing civilian targets in London—they liked creating panic in cities.

"There are posters everywhere in Madras now asking Indians to sign on as soldiers," periappa said.

Appa shook his head. "Unbelievable, isn't it?" he said. "They treat us like dirt, then expect us to die fighting under their command."

"I don't know why anyone signs up," periappa said. "They let our boys enlist, but keep them in the lowest rank and pay them next to nothing regardless of how smart or brave they are."

"Only white people have the brains to be officers," appa said. "We are too stupid, of course." He laughed mirthlessly, and periappa joined him in a rare moment of agreement.

After appa turned the old Murphy off, I went to my room, yawning. Amma entered as I was tucking the edges of the white cotton mosquito net into my mattress. "Is everything all right, kanna?" she asked, her hand hovering hesitantly above the light switch, suspended in mid-motion. "You were very quiet today."

"I didn't know what to say."

"Is it something at school?" she asked with concern.

"No." I paused, struggling for words.

She stood waiting patiently.

"Amma," I said tentatively. "I don't want to get married."

"What, Vidya kanna?" Amma said anxiously.

"I mean, I don't want to get married until I finish school," I said nervously.

Amma's expression cleared a little. "Don't worry," she said. "I'm sure we can wait a little longer. After all, girls are getting married much later these days. Even seventeen is not considered too old anymore."

I smiled with relief. I wondered whether to bring up college but decided to wait. There was no point asking for too much. Amma had agreed to a year's reprieve at least, so I had months to think about how to ask for more time. Maybe Kitta would help me with that.

Amma stepped close to me and touched my cheek through the mesh of the net. Her palm was warm and dry, as always. Her fingers carried the faint scent of the saffron spice she had cooked with. "You mustn't worry. Marriage is a wonderful thing." She turned out the light and left.

The rain was no more than a drizzle now, stirring up the smell of moist mud, which wafted in through the open window. I heard Raja whine softly, still tied to a pillar on the back verandah. He wasn't happy.

Even dogs prefer freedom, I thought.

Black Crow

The next morning, I was watching the dust in my room float aimlessly in the cone of sunshine streaming in through the window when appa opened the door a crack and peeped in. I sat up on my bed at once and stretched my arms upward until they touched the mosquito net.

"Sorry. Did I wake you?" he asked.

"No," I replied.

"Would you like to come with me to drop periappa off? I'm driving him to the station."

I nodded.

"You need to get ready soon. We leave in about half an hour," he said.

I splashed cold water on my face and brushed my teeth. Periappa was eating breakfast so noisily that I could hear him slurping and crunching as soon as I stepped out of my room.

Kitta was still sleeping, which pleased me. I hardly ever got time to be alone with appa these days.

Appa lifted periappa's steel trunk into the backseat, and I sat beside it. Amma handed me a basket with a long brass tiffin box full of food for periappa's trip back to Madras. Periappa sat in front, talking about Malati's marriage and what appa should be doing about mine.

I tried to ignore what periappa was saying. The road left Mahim, where we lived, and wound through Breach Candy, the white section of the city. Rifka said there were signs at the Breach Candy club and swimming pool that said "Indians and dogs not allowed." I hadn't seen the signs myself, but it was obvious we weren't welcome—the only Indian people I could see were the watchmen at the gates.

As the car came closer to Victoria station, brown faces surrounded us, and I only saw a few dots of white in the crowd. The station was bustling with activity even early in the morning: sweaty, muscular rickshaw wallahs, pulling their fares behind them; hawkers peddling carts heaped with different types of bananas and mangoes; beggars hunched over and dressed in rags, whining, "Paise, sahib? Coins, sir?"

Pink-skinned British families picked their way to their whites-only first-class compartments through the seething mass of Indians who swarmed across the platform like ants on an anthill, thronging around the third-class carriages. Coolies in red uniforms were shouting at the tops of their voices, and appa allowed one of them to carry periappa's luggage for a few paise—saying that after all, they earned very little for all the hard work they did.

"You are much too simple," periappa said. "You give too much to these people. Your servants rule your home too, I could tell that. Away all weekend, they were."

Appa ignored him and set the trunk on the round circle of cloth that the coolie had placed on his head like a tiny turban. As I jostled through the crowd, I accidentally brushed against a British girl at least a head shorter than I was.

Something rapped me on my shins and I winced. The white girl, in a frilly pink dress gathered at the waist and tied behind her in a fancy bow, had hit me with her parasol.

"Don't touch me, blackie!" Her lips curled back in a snarl. "Look where you're going, you crow!" she spat.

I stared at her openmouthed. Her mother looked past me, wrinkling her nose as though I were a heap of dung. "Come along, darling. Don't mind that coolie girl. There won't be any coloreds in our compartment," she said.

"We aren't all coolies!" I yelled as loudly as I could.

I saw heads turn to see who had shouted, but appa held me firmly by my elbow and steered me away. "Let it go, Vidya," he said under his breath.

I could feel anger, bitter as bile, in my mouth. Why didn't he stick up for me? Periappa didn't slow his steps.

We reached periappa's carriage, and the coolie dropped his

trunk on the dusty red floor beneath the wooden slats of the lowest berth. People were pressing into the carriage, crushing me as I walked out and stood on the platform, watching appa and periappa talk. A whistle blew. Periappa said something I didn't catch, and I didn't bother to tell him to greet Malati or periamma or any of the others on my behalf.

The steam engine spewed clouds of black smoke into the faraway metal arches of the station's vaulted ceiling. Then the wheels began to turn, and the stationmaster waved his green flag. The great clock at the end of the station chimed eight times. A magnified voice boomed over the megaphone and the great iron beast pulled out, huffing.

We walked away from the station's smells of sweat and smoke and ripe fruit and got into the Austin in silence. "How can you let them insult me?" I burst out, slamming the door shut. "You're supposed to be a freedom fighter."

As soon as I said it, I realized I'd crossed the limit. "Sorry, appa," I mumbled.

I glanced at my father, but I could not read his facial expression. He revved up the engine and waited as a cow ambled across the road, chewing its cud lazily.

"Vidya, there are different ways to fight." His voice was gentle.

"They think we're cowards for taking their insults lying down like doormats," I said. "They don't respect us for shutting up. That girl looked at me as if I were a cockroach she'd like to squash."

"And should I have raised my hand against her?" appa asked. "A girl too young to think for herself?"

"You could have told her stupid parents something."

"Stoop to their level? Call them white termites? Is that what you would have liked me to do?"

"Yes! It would have been a lot better than staying as quiet as a crushed cockroach," I said stubbornly.

He shook his head. "Dignity, Vidya. That's what we need to keep. Don't you know the Tamil proverb? If a dog barks at the sun, it does not dim the sun's brightness."

"They don't even notice when you hold back," I said. "What's the point fighting in a way they don't respect?"

"They'll learn from us, Vidya, slowly. We set an example the world will follow."

"If you're so proud of it, then why do you sneak off on your own?" I demanded. "Why don't you take us with you? I want to see a protest march too."

He looked at me for a moment before turning his eyes on the road again. "It isn't safe."

I banged the dashboard with my fist. "You won't let me do anything," I shouted. "You talk about freedom and you won't give me any. You just want me to get married so you can wash your hands of me. I'm going to run away."

I was shocked to hear him laugh. "Where will you go?"

"Maybe I'll join some freedom fighters," I said seriously.

"All right, then," he said, smiling.

"All right?" I asked, surprised.

"Yes, if you like, but why don't you wait a bit?" He was still smiling.

"Wait for what?"

"Wait until you finish college."

"What?" I could feel a foolish grin cutting across my face.

He turned his eyes away from the road for a moment to look at me. "Just don't tell your mother yet, okay? I'll tell her myself. Later."

"Can I go to college, appa? Really?" I'd never imagined it would be this easy.

"Really." He had a satisfied look, the kind of look he always had after he gave me my birthday present every year.

I threw my arms around his neck. "Careful. I'm driving," he said.

The salt air of the beach floated in through the open window. I wanted to shout, laugh, cry with joy all at the same time.

"Happy?" he asked.

"More," I said. "More than happy. *Much* more than just happy."

How much time had I spent needlessly worrying about

college? I stared ahead dreamily. At night, the arc of the city sparkled so much that it was nicknamed the queen's necklace. In the morning, it was no more than a lot of tall buildings standing straight as soldiers, but even the plain old buildings looked suddenly beautiful to me.

"Appa," I said, "how did you know I wanted to go to college?"

"You don't give me much credit, do you? I've seen you every day for the last fifteen years." He laughed, and I joined in.

"So which college do you want to go to?" he asked.

"I don't know, really." Oddly, I'd never given it much thought before. College seemed so unlikely that I'd never bothered to imagine what I'd like to study or where.

Right then, it didn't even matter. I felt as light as a sunbeam. I was going to college somewhere to study something. That was enough for the moment.

The joyous clamor in my mind drowned out the strange sound outside the car: a humming noise that was gathering speed and growing louder, a roar that was not the waves curling up the beach.

The Protest March

Appa saw the crowd approaching. He pulled the car over to the side of the road and stopped. I looked at him quizzically, and he pointed.

People were marching toward us, a wall of people stretching from one end of the road to the other, filling it and spreading across both sides of the pavement, an endless mass of humanity. We could not possibly drive the car through that crowd. "Appa, is that a protest march?" I asked with excitement.

"Yes." He sounded somewhat concerned. "I didn't know they were coming this way."

I could hear their chants clearly now. "*Jai Hind!* Victory to India! Jai Hind! Victory to India!"

The bright, banned Indian tricolor flag was flapping in the sea breeze—saffron, white and green. "Freedom!" a banner proclaimed in English, Hindi and Marathi.

I watched as the flood of people came closer and closer like a rising tide. Our Austin was no more than a tiny pebble in the river of protestors who flowed around us.

"Stay inside the car, Vidya," appa said warningly, but I had already pried the door open. I stared up at a few faces, but no one made eye contact. Everyone was looking straight ahead fixedly, shouting slogans or waving flags.

As I emerged out of the car and immersed myself in the crowd, they began to sing the Indian national song, "Vande Mataram." It was a song the British had banned.

"Victory to our nation!" I shouted as loudly as I could, moving a few steps away from the car. "Jai Hind! Victory to our nation!"

Appa was watching me with a mixture of anxiety and amusement. I wanted to shout, "I'm going to college!" but that would have been inappropriate.

"We should go before amma gets worried," he said, but we couldn't. The Austin was stranded, like a beached whale. We were caught there, caught until the crowd melted away. It felt like a party. Before appa could say any more, I plunged farther in.

"Vidya!" appa shouted as I was jostled away from him by the crowd. The amusement had drained out of his face. He looked scared. "Stay close to me!"

I could barely see the top of his head. The mass of bodies between us grew thicker. I pretended I hadn't heard. At last I was a part of something important and immense. I walked farther away from him.

"Vidya! Get back here!" Appa's form was lost far behind

me. His voice was nearly drowned by the chanting. Protestors seethed around me, and I did not feel the heat of the sun on my head nor the sweat that was starting to trickle down the back of my blouse. I wanted it to go on forever.

I couldn't hear appa's firm footsteps following me. When he reached me, his grip was almost painful on my elbow, forcing me to stop, pushing me closer to the pavement. I struggled to move forward, fighting him.

Then in the distance, I heard another sound. The sound of hooves. The smell of horse sweat mingling with the acrid scent of melting tar.

I liked horses. I wanted to see the mounted police. I turned around eagerly.

The crowd had stopped moving. It was a terrible stillness—as though the sea had suddenly frozen.

"Kneel!" someone cried. "The horses won't trample us."

"Let them come! I'll never kneel before the British," another voice rang out.

Confused shouts cut through the tense air. A mounted British officer appeared and hurled out orders in a heavily accented Hindi that I hardly understood.

People were standing arm in arm, huddled together in groups or linking elbows in long chains. There was fear on some faces, anger on others, but all of them stood straight, like a grove of Ashoka trees. The brightly colored saris of a few women peeped like scattered blossoms between the drab white kurthas of the men. Their voices rose again and a Hindi song, "Sare Jahan Se Acha," trembled into the air.

As the song hung there, shivering with fear and anticipation, khaki-clad policemen charged into the crowd, their lathi sticks raised. The crisp foreign accent calling out commands in broken Hindi was coming closer.

Then I saw her. A woman with beautiful hair gathered in a glistening, thick braid that slithered down to her waist like a black cobra. I saw the veins pulsing on her neck and on her forehead. I saw the muscles flex in her arms as she lifted the tricolor flag, high, high above her head.

An Indian policeman waved his lathi at her, hesitating.

"Teach her a lesson, you squeamish fool!" the white officer on the horse yelled. "Whose side are you on?"

"Yes, sir!" the Indian policeman said, but instead of beating the woman, he turned to rain his blows down on another man.

"*Ullu ka baccha!* Son of a prostitute!" the mounted policeman cursed. The swearwords sounded strange in the officer's foreign mouth.

I heard the staccato clop of horse hooves, louder now. His stallion neighed as though in protest before the officer stooped down, his lathi landing across the woman's shoulders with a thwack. Her song was suffocated like a lamp snuffed out in a sudden wind.

The sari slipped off her shoulder and I turned away, but not before I heard the ripping sound as the officer's worm white fingers curled around her exposed blouse. I saw the immodesty of her suddenly uncovered breasts. A boy not much taller than I ran toward her, screaming incoherently.

Appa strode down the street. He lifted the lady's limp body in his arms, bending over her protectively. Blows began to fall onto his broad shoulders from the white officer's lathi.

Appa was strong. He was tall. He could have pulled the officer down off the horse, thrown him on the ground and kicked him. But he did not.

I saw the officer's arm, with its curly yellow hair, coming down, down, down on my father's head, on his neck, on his back.

Appa's blood began to creep across his light Lucknow kurtha—bright, angry, fresh and red. Not the tired rusty stain of someone else's blood. Then the lathi hit Appa's skull again, with a sound like the priest cracking open a coconut at the temple—the sound of my father's final sacrifice.

The Idiot

Appa crumpled, falling to earth slowly like an uprooted Ashoka tree. It seemed an age before he hit the ground. The woman he was carrying fell from his arms in a dead faint, lying on the road beside him, her feet intertwined with his. Blood burst from their clothes like red lotus buds opening.

I stood in the middle of the road like a statue. I heard my own voice, unrecognizably hoarse, crying, "Appa, appa, appa." I could not walk toward him—toward the twisted mess that my father's strong body had become.

Vans arrived, white, with bold red letters proclaiming that they were the police. I watched the crowd being herded into the vans like cattle. They went willingly. They thronged around the vans, those who could still walk or hobble, waiting to get in and go to jail. The vans were packed with people squashed together like mangoes in a pickle jar. They drove away stuffed full of nonviolent protestors.

The street was empty now except for a few men, a few women. Those who had been left behind for lack of space. And those others whose bodies lay crumpled on the smoldering tar road, whose blood dribbled into its black crevices.

Someone, a man in a Muslim skullcap with a finely trimmed beard—a man as large as my father—began to drag appa away. I ran after him, repeating the only word that remained in my mouth, "Appa, appa."

The tar lay in molten pools in the midday heat. My left slipper stuck to it and came off. I did not stop running though my bare sole burned.

Then a pair of strong arms scooped me up as though I were a child and a soothing voice said, "We're going to help him. Don't worry."

We entered a tent with many wounded men. My father's form was spread out flat on a stretcher. Blood was seeping onto the floor. I could not recognize the lopsided lump of flesh and bone that had once formed his face.

"He's alive," someone said. *He's alive, he's alive,* the words throbbed in my brain with hope.

Doctors were attending to my father. I had never seen that before. I thought, stupidly, Sometimes doctors need other doctors. One of them walked toward me, a lemon yellow sari peeping incongruously from beneath her dirty once-white overcoat.

No hospitals, no ambulances because if appa went to a hospital, he could be jailed by the British, she said. Did I understand? The vast majority of freedom fighters were sent to prison without trial. Their courts were unfair even if a case ever went to court. Did I understand?

I nodded.

There was a makeshift hospital that had been set up in someone's home. They would take him there and care for him.

"What's your name, child? Where do you live?" the doctor asked.

I must have told them my address. I must have pointed to the car that still stood, miraculously unscathed and incongruous, in the middle of the empty road. Someone must have driven me back because then I was at home. My mother held me close, and I could hear her heartbeat and smell her sandalwood soap and talcum powder. I heard a man's voice telling my mother, "Your daughter is all right, madam, but your husband is hurt badly."

I heard my mother's painful silence as we staggered up the stairs to the home of the old couple who lived in the flat above. I swayed on my feet, and Kitta slipped his arm around my shoulders. Their maid gasped when she saw us, but the old couple walked up and invited us in.

"My husband has been hurt," amma said. "May I leave the children with you for a few days?" Then she was gone.

The old couple insisted that we eat, and I remember my surprise that I could feel hungry in spite of all that had happened.

That Kitta and I could remember to murmur our thanks for their kindness.

Before I fell into the soft white bed in the room Kitta and I were sharing until my mother's return, they let Raja in. He came up to me slowly, his tail drooping, as though he realized that something had gone seriously wrong. He placed his moist nose on my knee, and I slept with my hands buried in his warm fur.

A fortnight later, when the person who was only the empty shell of my father walked back into our lives, Raja did not jump up to lick him. He could tell, when appa finally returned, walking but not talking, with the same old body but with no mind in it anymore, that it no longer really was appa.

My father's brain had been crushed in a way no doctor could set right again. He was an idiot now and would be until the day his body died too.

Ganesha Chathurthi

My mother didn't force me to go to school again. I was thankful. I didn't want to see my friends, not even Rifka, my closest confidant. I did not want to tell them the truth. A martyr I could have explained to my friends; an idiot I could not.

Rifka called the day my father returned.

"It's Rifka," amma said. "Talk to her, kanna. You should talk to someone."

I forced myself to walk to the phone. "Hello, Rifka," was all I was able to say.

"Are you ill?" Rifka asked. "You haven't been to school for ages."

I wanted to speak to Rifka, but I couldn't.

"What's going on, Vidya? Your mother's voice sounded awful. Are you all down with pneumonia?"

I had a sudden urge to laugh hysterically. Or cry hysterically. Or do both. Instead, I tried to answer. "No. We're not all ill. We—my father—" I choked.

"Vidya, talk to me, please," Rifka pleaded. "Did something happen to your father?"

"Yes." A word was all I could manage.

"Did they jail him? Did they hurt him?" She sounded worried.

"Yes," I whispered into the receiver. "They hurt him."

"What happened? How is he? Can my dad help?"

"No," I said.

"Can't you talk to me about it?"

"I want to," I said, struggling to find words. "I want to," I repeated.

Rifka waited patiently, but I fell silent again. "Is he badly hurt?" she asked at last.

"It's hopeless. No one can do anything to make him right again." It was the first time I had voiced the fact aloud.

"Let us come over, Vidya. Please." She sounded scared.

I wanted to see Rifka, but I couldn't bear the thought of her seeing appa the way he was. I remembered the admiration that had shone in her eyes when she had called him a hero. She would be shocked, horrified. I wouldn't let that happen to her.

"No," I said. "I can't let you come over. Don't. Please don't. We just need to be alone as a family. You're still my best friend, but we just can't have you over right now."

"Then please come here and see us for a bit. You should spend some time outside your house with me. It'll help."

"I can't," I said.

She was quiet.

"Are you angry?" I asked.

"Angry?" She sounded surprised. "No, of course not." Her voice became gentler. "I understand. Or at least, I really am trying to. Okay? I just wish I could help somehow. That we could do something for your family."

"Thanks for understanding," I murmured. "I wish I could talk more, but I can't." I didn't want to think of all that had happened.

"Just rest and get better soon, yes?" she said gently.

"Yes."

"We're friends forever and ever, you know that, don't you?" she finished.

"Yes," I said. "Thank you." The phone went dead, and my voice died with it. I didn't feel like saying anything more, not even to Kitta.

Amma didn't understand my need for silence as well as Kitta and Rifka did. "You must talk, kanna," she said several times. "It will be a lot better if you tell us what happened. You're safe now."

But how could I bring myself to tell her that I was responsible for what had happened to appa? That if I had not run away from the car, if I had listened to him, he would still be with us? What would she say if she knew what I had done?

Amma's brother, Bala maama, came all the way from his home in Coimbatore to stay with us for a few weeks. He came to help amma with the finances, with managing the household. Amma had never even been to the bank or operated an account—appa had taken care of everything that had to do with money. He had earned; he had paid the rent; he had taken care of the salaries for our domestic staff.

Bala maama and amma spent a lot of time together, talking in low voices. Sometimes Kitta sat in on their discussions, but I never did.

One morning, after breakfast, when I was about to leave the table, amma laid a hand on my wrist.

"Vidya, we need to talk," she said. "All of us."

I sat down again listlessly.

"I can't pay the rent here," amma said softly. "Or the school fees. So we have to make some changes."

"But amma, we have savings," Kitta said. "Appa was careful, wasn't he? Bala maama said we had savings."

She looked at him unhappily. "We have some money in the bank, Kitta," she said. "Enough to pay for your college and enough to give Vidya a good dowry. She'll need a good dowry, especially now," she added, lowering her voice.

"I can earn," Kitta said. "I can get a job."

"You need to complete your education," amma said sharply. "You know that."

Bala maama nodded vigorously. "You must finish college, Kitta," he said.

"Anyway, no one can live off savings forever," amma said. "We need a steady income, and I can't earn." All her life, she had been trained to be a housewife. She had no education. She wasn't qualified for any kind of job.

"You can't live here without a man in the house," Bala maama added.

Kitta opened his mouth as though to object, and then he shut it wordlessly.

"Your grandfather suggested that we move to Madras and live with the rest of your father's family," amma continued. "Your father's father and your father's brothers are duty bound to support us if we join their household. We can't burden anyone else with our upkeep."

My voice was hoarse with unspoken words.

"I would gladly have you in our home," Bala maama interjected. "But it would not be right for you to stay with us."

"My place is with my husband's family," amma said flatly. "A married woman must stay at her husband's home."

Kitta reached out across the table and took my hand. My palm was limp, but he squeezed hard, and then he walked over and laid his arm across my shoulders. My body sagged against his upright torso.

Appa sat silently in the dining room with us as he always did these days—like a shell cast up on the beach after the crab within had died. I looked at him. He stared back, his eyes empty of recognition. There was a bandage across his forehead still, and his arm was in a sling. He moaned softly.

All my fault. The words were now a ceaseless wail in my head.

"Are you okay, Vidya?" amma asked gently.

I looked away. I did not even have enough voice left to cry.

Amma never cried either. At least, I never saw her break down. When our servants came to say good-bye, she gave a present to each of them. Ponni sobbed loudly, and amma tried to comfort her.

After they left, amma helped me pack my things for the move to Madras.

"We can't take much," amma said. "Maybe just your favorite books?"

I shook my head. I didn't remember which my favorite books were anymore.

"Shall I pack for you, kanna?" amma asked.

I nodded listlessly.

Amma put her jewelry away. The watery sound of golden bangles that used to flow on amma's wrist was silenced. The diamond sparkle disappeared from her earlobes. It had long since disappeared from the depths of her dark eyes.

Bala maama forced her to wear her plain gold ear studs. "It's not like you're a widow," he said to her firmly. "You're still young. You don't have to stop wearing jewelry."

"What's the point?" she said to him. "He doesn't know me anymore. Better to save them for Vidya."

I wanted to tell her that I didn't want jewels, that I never liked jewelry. But I couldn't speak.

"One day, when you are a bride, you will wear them," amma said, packing them away. Her eyelids were puffy and red.

❧

The festival of Ganesha Chathurthi came late that year, a few weeks before our departure in late September. Bala maama insisted that we should celebrate it.

"Your husband is still alive," he told amma. "You are not in mourning."

He bought us a clay idol of Ganesha, the elephant god, remover of obstacles, content with himself despite his bulky body and bachelorhood, who rested his giant frame on a tiny mouse as a constant reminder that miracles could happen.

Amma sanctified the diety in our poojai room and worshipped him for three days. I watched but did not join her.

On the third day, we took him to the beach. Crowds of people were there, drowning idols of Ganesha in the ocean, a reminder that all things were transitory.

Amma handed me our clay idol. "Things will be better soon," amma said. "All troubled times end. I know you are hurting, Vidya, but even this pain is transitory."

I wanted to tell her that some things were permanent. I had been thoughtless for a few minutes, and those minutes had changed our lives forever.

I hurled our Ganesha idol as far as I could with all of my strength. We watched it arc through the air and sink into the ocean.

Madras

Our last night in Bombay, I let Raja into my room, and he sat at the foot of my bed, and I buried my hands in the smooth hair of his neck all night long. He knew it was good-bye, but he did not whine. He licked me every now and then.

The next morning, I called Rifka.

"Vidya!" she exclaimed, sounding delighted. "I was scared to phone and disturb you. I knew you'd call as soon as things were okay again. It's so wonderful to hear your voice. I've missed you so much. When are you coming back to school?"

"Never," I said.

I could feel her shock in the eloquent silence that traveled across the telephone wire. "What?" she asked at last, somewhat feebly. "Aren't things better?"

"No," I said. My voice seemed emotionless. "Things have changed. Completely."

"It's been so long since I saw you. Can I come over now?"

"Rifka, we're leaving for Madras today," I said. "I wanted to let you know earlier, but I just couldn't. It was too difficult."

"Why?" she asked, shocked. "What happened? How long will be you gone? When do you leave?"

I couldn't find the energy to answer all her questions. "I'll write to you," I said.

"I'll miss you." Rifka paused. "Vidya, what's happening? Tell me. Please. I want to help."

"My dad was hurt. I told you that, didn't I? He can't work anymore. So we have to move to Madras to stay with my grandfather."

"You're going to live in that extended family house forever?"

"Yes," I said. "We don't have a choice."

Rifka lapsed again into a stunned silence. "I can't believe it," she said finally. "I am so sorry. When do you leave? Maybe we can come to the station and see you off?"

"I don't want you to see my father, Rifka, please. I'll explain it later, but I just couldn't take that. I'll write from Madras. I'll write everything in a letter."

"All right," she said softly. "I'll be waiting to hear from you."

"Thanks, Rifka. I'll miss you. A lot." I hung up.

Bala maama took us to the station, sending us on our way to appa's family. He stroked Raja's head before we left the house.

"Don't worry about him," he said to me. "I'll look after him well until you can have him again." I tried to smile. I wanted to thank Bala maama for pretending we weren't leaving forever.

But the conversation with Rifka had drained me, and I said nothing.

Bala maama carried our suitcases into our compartment and stood on the platform until the train began to move.

Kitta gave me the window seat without fighting for it. I looked out as the train meandered through the emerald ranges of the Ghats. Sometimes a bit of coke flew into my eye from the coal engine, but I didn't turn to ask amma to blow it out. I waited instead until the wind blew the piece away, and my eyes filled with tears, but the tears did not reach my throat and tear out the frozen feeling. I still could not cry.

The signs on the station platforms turned from Hindi to scripts I did not recognize and then finally into Tamil. I remembered how appa had once written my name in six different Indian languages—all the scripts he had mastered. He sat between amma and Kitta now, moaning softly once in a great while.

There was no one to receive us when we arrived at the Madras station, our clothes caked with coal dust and grimy with sweat.

We boarded a long red bus and collapsed onto the faded vinyl seats. They felt different from the soft, cushioned seats of the Austin. The bus smelled sweaty.

Appa slept, his head lolling against Kitta's shoulder. The bandages were gone now, but his head was bruised and misshapen. People stared at him and pointed and whispered.

The bus bumped along the potholed roads, past small tea shops, large redbrick government buildings, and spacious bungalows. There were no multistory residences in Madras, though they were common in Bombay.

The bus overtook a *jutka,* a covered horse-drawn cart, before lumbering to a stop in front of a large temple. The conductor announced the stop, "Mylapore." I stared at the intricately carved *gopuram,* the temple cupola.

"This is where we get off," amma reminded. The crowd parted as we made our way out. I got off the bus and almost walked into a man pushing along a cart piled high with melons.

"Come, kanna," amma said. I trailed behind her and appa. Kitta led the way through the narrow, noisy streets.

Then we were standing, the four of us, behind the low, whitewashed wall, staring at the great yellow house with its flat concrete roof under which our family's fate would be fused with that of appa's brothers' families: periappa, periamma and Malati; appa's two younger brothers and their wives, Chinni chithi and Sarasa chithi, and their children. Appa had one sister, but she had moved out long ago to live with her husband's family. My grandfather, thatha, was the patriarch of the household; my grandmother had died in childbirth years ago, before I was born.

The dark, pointed leaves of a mango tree brushed up against the house from behind. The front door was open. Within was a dark cave of space—large, empty halls furnished with nothing but straw mats—no tables, no chairs—though thatha was rich enough to afford them. Thatha believed that Brahmins were supposed to lead simple lives. To him, that meant we had to have as few material possessions as possible.

I opened the creaky gate. Amma followed, holding appa by the hand. I looked at him, wondering if his face would register some sign of recognition, but it didn't. Kitta closed the gate and we pulled our suitcases up the front stairs.

My grandfather emerged on the verandah. I stared at him. In all the summers we had spent in this house, he had never once come down to receive us. He was usually holed away in his study. He hardly ever communicated directly, especially with his daughters-in-law.

"Welcome," thatha said, reaching a hand toward his son. "Venkat, welcome home."

Appa's eyes passed over his form dully.

"He doesn't recognize any of us," amma whispered. "He never speaks."

Thatha dropped appa's hand abruptly and turned to my mother. "Welcome," he said. "This house is your home now."

I said nothing. His words were my prison sentence. I clamped my teeth down on my lower lip to keep from screaming.

Thatha looked past us to our shabby suitcases. "Did no one come to the station?"

"They were no doubt busy," amma said.

"Someone should have been there to receive you," thatha said.

"It was not necessary," amma repeated. "You should not have troubled yourself to come down."

Thatha didn't reply. Instead, he said to Kitta, "I have seen to it about your college. You can continue your studies at the Madras University." He plucked up one of the suitcases and entered the house.

Kitta pressed my hand and we stepped in behind thatha. We entered the main hall, with stairs leading off to the right and three small rooms on the left: the poojai room, a tiny private bedroom and the small hall where men gathered in the evenings. We parted ways. Kitta turned right and led my father's silent form up the stairs that were forbidden to us women. They would live above, in the men's realm, with my uncles and my grandfather, with access to the breezy terrace that appa had once told me about.

Before, I had hated to see appa and Kitta go up those stairs every summer, to be parted from both of them for two months—but I had always known then that there would be an end. There would be the train ride back home when we could all laugh together, crunching pieces of cashew brittle and sipping chai in earthenware cups sold by some hawker. Laugh about the craziness of this house without being too disrespectful.

I waited until they disappeared before I followed amma through the main hall into the dining room, which was directly after it, and then left, into the long room where the women slept.

Chinni chithi, my youngest aunt, turned at the sound of our footsteps, holding her hands out to my mother.

"Welcome," she said softly.

She was the wife of appa's youngest brother, the one who had torn out of my grandmother's body in so great a hurry that she had bled to death after his birth. Chinni chithi had a frail, bent body; her hair was limp and skinny as a rat's tail. A starved rat at that.

Sarasa chithi, my second aunt, wife of my father's second brother, saw us but pretended not to and hurried away to the kitchen. She was tall and thin, like a sharp spear ready to pierce into flesh. She always sucked up to periamma, the woman who ordered the rest of us about as though she were queen and we her servants. If I had any doubts as to whether periamma was pleased about our arrival, Sarasa chithi's behavior set them at rest.

"Did you have a good train trip?" Chinni chithi asked.

I forced a smile but let amma reply. "Yes," amma said politely. "It was very pleasant."

"I made a place for you," Chinni chithi said shyly, showing us the corner of the great steel cabinet where we would keep our possessions.

I was almost glad then that we had brought so little. There was no place for books.

"Here is a new mat for you," Chinni chithi said, handing me the tightly rolled-up straw mat on which I would sleep.

"Chinni!" periamma's voice echoed in the room through the long dining hall, audible all the way from the kitchen.

"It's dinnertime," Chinni chithi said, and scuttled away like a frightened mouse.

"Ah, there you are," periamma said when she saw me. "Wash your hands and help serve the men." The men always ate first in this house, and the women served them. On normal days, it was only during mealtimes that the genders met.

I looked at the way periamma's stomach peeped out and rolled over the pleats of her sari—like a *podalanga,* a misshapen water gourd. She turned her back to me, the ugliest back of anyone I'd seen, with two strange folds of flesh dangling down from her shoulders like misplaced breasts.

I lifted the pot of sambhar without saying a word. It was heavy.

"Don't spill a drop," periamma warned.

I said nothing.

"What's the matter?" she asked. "Become an idiot like your father? Lost your voice too?"

My voice came lashing out like a whip. "He's not an idiot," I cried.

"Of course he is. Go! The men are waiting," she replied.

I clenched my fists. I would give that stupid old witch what she deserved. How dare she call my father an idiot?

Amma looked up at me pleadingly. "Please, kanna," she begged. Her eyes were pinkish red. "Please don't make any trouble."

Something about her voice silenced me. It made me feel suddenly as though she were a child and I the mother. I wanted to reach out and hug her.

I struggled to squash the tears that were rising in my throat and ducked out of the doorway before they could spill out. The sambhar sloshed dangerously close to the surface of the pot.

"The idiot can sit in the corner," periappa was saying. How could he call his own brother an idiot? Appa was staring at the wall sightlessly. Kitta sat beside him. He didn't react to what periappa had said. Didn't anyone else care how they referred to appa anymore, even if he was just an empty shell?

"I can feed him," Kitta said to amma. "Don't worry."

Amma returned to the kitchen. Periamma went ahead of me, with the steaming pot of rice. She heaped four large spoonfuls onto periappa's silver plate and shook a tiny portion off the spoon onto Kitta's.

I had seen how much food there was in the kitchen. Thatha didn't spend as lavishly as appa had done, and everyone in this

house led a relatively ascetic lifestyle, but we weren't poor. Periamma was just trying her best to show how much our presence
displeased her.

"May I have some more, please?" Kitta asked.

Periamma glared at him and shook a few more grains off the
serving spoon. I looked in thatha's direction. Was he really so
oblivious to what was going on?

"More, please?" Kitta asked again.

I smiled sweetly at periamma and raised my voice. "Well,
periamma, are you going to serve him some more or shall I?"

"Is something the matter?" thatha asked, looking at me,
mildly perturbed.

"I was just about to serve Kitta some more rice," periamma
said. "He eats a lot."

"He's a growing boy," thatha said. "Perhaps he'll become as
tall as his father."

I gave Kitta a triumphant look as periamma gave him his
second serving. Amma appeared by my side, carrying the curry.
"Please," she said in an undertone. "Please behave. We're guests
here."

"Oh, really?" I said. "I was under the mistaken impression
we're family."

"I see my sister found her voice," Kitta said, smiling but
keeping his voice low.

I couldn't help but glance back at Kitta with a crescent of

a half smile. I filled the ladle with sambhar and sloshed three spoonfuls onto his plate. It was lucky the plate had a rim, or it would have spilled onto the floor and periamma would probably have slapped me silly.

"Please. Don't make it uncomfortable." Amma's voice was hoarse, as though she had a sore throat.

"Never thought we'd end up in a Dickensian orphanage," Kitta said softly. "I might as well be Oliver Twist."

I moved on to ladle some sambhar onto the plate of the man who had once been my father.

After the men were done with their meal, amma walked appa to the tap and rinsed his hands and his mouth as though he were a child. She stroked his hair and touched his cheek with her long fingers. I caught myself waiting to see some response from appa's side, but there was nothing. Then Kitta led him away again.

The women sat down, the wives taking the places where their husbands had sat.

Did amma still love the man who used to be my father? Or was it just the dry ash of duty still smoldering in her breast? Did I still love what remained of him?

My cousin Malati's voice cut through my thoughts.

"Do you know that I've already been chosen?" she asked.

"Yes, I heard," I answered. "Periappa told us you were to be married when he visited."

"Last year, at our cousin Kamakshi's wedding, there was a boy who saw me, and he was so entranced by my beauty that he asked his parents to ask my parents for my hand in marriage," Malati continued smugly. "He was so keen on our alliance they didn't even want to get our horoscopes matched."

"Oh," I said. Entranced by her beauty, indeed. I would have been horrified if it had happened to me.

Malati flashed her ravishing dark eyes in anger at me for not expressing more excitement about her engagement. "Are you jealous?" she demanded.

I'd never thought Malati could make me laugh. "Do I look jealous to you?"

She glared. "Of course you are. I can see you're trying to hide it. Poor you. No one will marry you because your father is a fool."

"He's not a fool," I said. "He was very intelligent. The most intelligent man in this family. Then the British beat him and smashed his brain."

"My father would never be so foolish as to try and battle the British," she said sanctimoniously.

"Too bad," I said, putting an end to any possibility that we might ever strike up a friendship. "If the British had beaten your father, at least he would be no worse off than he is now. He has no brains to lose."

Malati got up and whined to her mother, "Vidya was rude to me!"

Periamma reached over at once and boxed my ear. "Don't you dare insult my daughter," she said.

Amma threw a caring glance in my direction. I shrugged nonchalantly, ignoring the ringing in my ear, pretending for amma's sake that my ear wasn't hurting.

I felt hungry for the first time in a long while, but thatha was nowhere nearby, and I was only doled out tiny portions of food under periamma's watchful, froglike eyes. "Too bad your greedy brother ate so much," she said, looking at me triumphantly. "Now you'll have to curb your appetite."

"Kitta isn't greedy," I said. My mother's pleading eyes stopped me from adding, "You are."

Periamma ate a great deal, including all the portions she forbade others, and sucked her fingers dry, noisily, at the end of her meal. Panting like a dog, she heaved her great bulk up from the floor. "Clean the floor carefully, Vidya. I'll let you have it if bits of rice stick to my feet tomorrow morning."

She lumbered toward the communal bedroom. Sarasa chithi followed her after a few minutes. Her constant flattery of periamma helped ensure she didn't have to work as hard as her other two sisters-in-law. Amma and Chinni chithi stayed behind to help clean the dining hall and the kitchen.

"Vidya, you will be going to Malati's school tomorrow," amma said. "I've arranged that."

"Thanks, amma." I looked at her gratefully.

A brief smile flitted across amma's hollow cheeks. Her once-round face looked gaunt. It was my fault she looked that way. It was my fault we were not still in Bombay.

"Go lie down," I said to her. "Please rest, amma. I'll finish."

By the time I was done cleaning, the light had already been turned out in the women's sleeping hall. I felt my way along the wall until I found my mat in the corner. My three aunts and two female cousins, Malati and baby Mangalam, were already asleep. So was amma.

I unrolled my mat and gazed outside the window at a coconut palm, which was cackling in the warm wind, its tough, thick trunk supporting snakelike creepers. The moon was imprisoned behind its long, spiky leaves.

But as the night wore on, the silver-blue moonlight sneaked in through the spaces and touched me softly on my shoulder. It was a caressing and comforting touch, and I finally fell asleep, almost annihilated with exhaustion.

School

I awoke to the low moo of the milkman's cow—he was probably at someone else's house down the street, pulling silky white strands from pink teats into the metal milk vessel. I got up quickly. I knew my morning chores: it was an old routine, which I had been forced to follow every day of our earlier summer visits. I was to make sure the milkman didn't deceive us and mix water into the milk (which I was sure the polite old man in a white turban would never dream of doing). After that, I had to pick flowers for the morning prayer.

I stretched silently on the mat and yawned. A bullock cart was lumbering in the distance. I heard a bicycle bell and a soft thump as the newspaper landed on the verandah. Then the sound of water tinkling on the front steps as the maid washed them clean.

I hated the communal bathing room, where the women went together each morning—a dingy room, lit only by a tiny high window, in the dim back corner of the house. I never felt clean bathing the way I had to here: forced to wrap a thin cloth around me to keep me from displaying my anatomy to anyone else, all the while dipping my mug into a metal bucket of lukewarm water to pour over myself. I promised myself that I would always be the first one up, the first one to bathe, so I could do it in privacy. All last summer I had felt Malati's prying eyes on me, trying to see if my breasts were developing.

After my bath, I combed my hair and stepped out into the garden. This was the one morning chore I actually liked. A *koel* bird was singing lustily as I filled my basket with flowers and came into the house, the newspaper under my other arm. I set the basket down in the poojai room and started reading an article.

"That's what we need in this house—dogs and cats burying their snouts in the morning paper. Get to work and don't ever let me catch you reading it," periamma said.

"Just out of curiosity, am I a dog or a cat?" I asked, but periamma pretended she hadn't heard.

"Give me the paper," she demanded.

Before dropping it into her hand, I quickly scanned *The Hindu's* headlines. There was something about the Soviets calling for cooperative action in the war against Germany. The battle was always growing bigger. Hitler's forces had invaded Russia in summer, breaking a pact they had made with that country. Hitler didn't seem to pay attention to any piece of paper he signed or any rule he himself did not make.

Periamma closed her eyes as soon as she was satisfied that I had no access to the paper. With her pudgy fingers, she began rubbing the *rudraksha malai,* the Indian rosary, its beads like petrified raisins. Her voice rose in song. It was the only time there was something beautiful about her. Her voice was like a rich, dark, velvety navy blue. I wondered if appa could still perceive colors in his mutilated mind.

Amma was already in the kitchen when I arrived, churning the curd to make butter and ghee, fresh clarified butter. Chinni chithi was grinding coffee beans. A strong, rich aroma pervaded the room as hot water seeped through the grains. Periamma walked in just in time to save some of the smooth brown liquid for herself before the rest was served to the men.

If I was lucky, I would get the second decoction, the one my mother and younger aunts shared, the weak and pale brown liquid that emerged when water percolated through the beans for the second time. Then water would be poured through for a third time and the pale, straw-colored liquid (which looked more like urine than like coffee) would be served to the maids and the gardener in special aluminum tumblers—because they were not Brahmin, our vessels were kept far away from their polluting touch.

I thought about appa, who believed that the British had done their best to intensify caste differences so they could fracture our society; that by practicing caste, we played into the hands of our conquerors. How differently we had treated Ponni and Xavier and Suruve. Yet why had appa never spoken out against the mistreatment of servants when we came to this house in the summers?

At breakfast, I brightened a little, wondering what school would be like. "Do you have a volleyball team at school?" I asked Malati hopefully.

She looked scandalized. "Of course not. Girls don't play sports at my school. At least not us older students."

"No sports at all?"

"Not unless you want to play with the six-year-olds," she said primly.

I didn't ask any other questions about school, but I refused to let her squelch my enthusiasm. It would be good to get out of the house.

Periamma let a coin drop in my palm before I left. "Change for your bus fare," she said grudgingly.

"Would you like to braid my hair?" Malati asked me as we walked to the bus stop, a maid following us a safe distance behind to see that we came to no harm.

"Not really," I told her.

"Braid my hair," she said, "or I'll tell everyone in school about your father."

"I already said no," I said. "But I guess your brain is so slow that I need to repeat everything I say."

"Not as slow as your father's brain," Malati said smartly. I wanted to slap her.

Malati tried again after we climbed into the bus and we each paid the conductor our fare. "Here's your last chance," she said. "Carry my bag or I'll tell everyone about your father."

"Go ahead." I shrugged. "I'm not going to become your servant." I sat behind her even though there was an empty place at her side. We rode a short distance along the beach, which sparkled in the early morning light. The smell of dried fish wafted in through the open windows of the bus and nearly made me gag. I closed my eyes for a moment and thought of Mahim beach—one of the few sandy stretches on the otherwise rocky Bombay coast—and the evening we had watched the sun falling into the waters of the Arabian Sea.

When we got to school, a flutter of anticipation darted through me. Our teacher, Mrs. Rao, made me stand in front of the whole class and say my name, where I was from and the name of the school I had been in. I flashed my best smile at her and scanned the classroom for a friendly face.

"My name is Vidya," I said brightly. "I came here from Walsingham Girls' School in Bombay."

Mrs. Rao did not smile back. Nor did any of the students.

"And what is your father?" she asked tersely.

The question confused me. What could she possibly mean?

"Well, I'm waiting," she said, raising her voice. "What is your father? Answer me at once."

"He's a man, of course, Mrs. Rao," I said nervously.

Giggles peppered the classroom. "I'm sorry." I tried to explain. "I was just confused. I wasn't trying to be smart."

Mrs. Rao stared right through me. "So you want to be the class clown?"

"No," I said earnestly. "I just didn't understand your question." The giggles turned into laughter.

"Are you trying to tell me my question was unclear?"

"Y-Yes," I stuttered. "I mean, no, ma'am."

"I will not tolerate this kind of behavior," Mrs. Rao said sternly. "Is that clear?"

"Yes, ma'am," I said as politely as I could.

But Mrs. Rao gave me detention for my impertinence anyway. "You will write down *I will not be impertinent* and *I will respect my elders* one hundred times in your notebook at lunchtime, and you're not going to eat until you're done; is that clear?"

"Very clear, Mrs. Rao," I said, still hoping to win her over with politeness.

She wasn't done with her questioning, however. "What does he do for a living, your father?"

I looked down at my feet silently.

"Is this question unclear too?"

"No, Mrs. Rao," I mumbled.

"Speak up, girl. What is your father's occupation?"

"He's dead," I blurted out. "He was part of a protest march. The British killed him."

I caught a few admiring glances from the girls. Malati made a movement as though to raise her hand, but I glared at her and she stopped bobbing in her seat. Instead, she waggled her finger at me, as though in warning.

Mrs. Rao wasn't impressed. "Sedition is a crime," she said. "Sounds like your father deserved to be put to death. Daughter of Mr. Good-for-nothing, I'll beat your spirit out of you if I have to. Your father should have done so before he died, but it appears he was remiss in all his duties."

The next morning, Malati managed to talk to Mrs. Rao before class began. Mrs. Rao was thrilled to find that she could make an example out of me.

"It has been brought to my attention that someone in the class is a liar," she said, caressing her long cane with her skinny fingers. "Now, who could that be?"

"Me," I said, and stood up. She didn't think I'd confess.

"Impertinent girl. Now, class, I will tell you the truth. This girl's father is not a freedom fighter at all. He is just an idiot. A madman. His brain doesn't function. Her cousin Malati informed me of this, unable to bear the lie that her cousin had told. I congratulate you, Malati. You were brave to tell me the truth. Clap your hands, class, to show your admiration for our honest Malati. Emulate her."

The class clapped loudly. Anything to miss a few minutes of Mrs. Rao's boring lecture, I thought.

"Now, Vidya, come forward," Mrs. Rao said, fondling her cane. "Which hand do you write with? No lying now. Your right. I see. Hold out your right hand, please."

The cane arced through the air, whistling, and came down, sending a stinging sensation through my entire arm. Once, twice, four times, eight times, and then the shooting pain made me lose count. I thought of appa, the white arm striking him repeatedly with a lathi, how much more that must have hurt. How had he managed to stay silent through the entire beating?

Don't cry, don't cry, don't cry, I thought. She caned my palm until it reddened. I thought she would make it bleed, but before that she tired. Lucky for me she wasn't angry enough to ignore the ache in her own arm.

"Be warned, girls," Mrs. Rao said, glowering as I returned to my seat. "Leopards don't change their spots. Vidya will always be a liar. Beware of her. Leave her alone. Keep the company of good girls like her cousin Malati, lest your own souls are corrupted."

None of the girls approached me after that. They were too frightened of Mrs. Rao.

After getting the morning off to a splendid start, Mrs. Rao gave us dictation and made sure I understood that I had to take it too.

I spelled every single word correctly. It was a small victory. Even Mrs. Rao couldn't fault me on my vocabulary.

Upstairs

That evening, after we returned from school, Malati announced that she didn't see the point of going to school anymore since she would be married in a few months anyway. Did she have to? she asked.

Periamma looked at her approvingly. "No, of course you don't. I'll speak to your father. You can stay home and perfect your cooking."

Malati looked delighted. I could not fathom the way her brain worked. What was it about getting married that made her so excited? I didn't want to think about it; she spent all her time thinking of nothing else.

I unrolled a bamboo mat that was in the corner of the women's hall and pulled out one of the short tables to serve as a writing desk. I sat cross-legged on the floor and began my homework.

Periamma turned on me at once. "How do you spend your time in the evenings?"

"What do you want me to do?" I said.

"You are to have music lessons with Malati's music teacher." My surprise must have shown because she was quick to clarify, "Thatha insisted on this. After music lessons and homework, you can mind Chinni's baby, Mangalam, until it is time for dinner. I don't want to hear a sound out of the baby. After dinner—"

I cut her short. "After dinner I have to clean up. I know. You don't have to tell me again."

"Don't talk back to me, ungrateful girl. With the mental faculties what they are in your family, I'm sure you did need reminding. We've saved your family from being turned out on the streets. Don't forget that for a moment."

I muttered under my breath that I was sure she would never let me forget, but then I saw the dark circles that hung beneath amma's eyes and I stopped guiltily.

I thought of Raja for a moment, the way his eyes had looked that last day in Bombay. Did he miss me? Who lived in our home now? Not a girl who climbed trees, I could be quite certain of that.

I went back to my homework. When it was done, I put the books away. I heard Malati's voice singing the scales and went to join her.

The music master sat cross-legged, facing Malati and me, the undersides of his callused feet peeping at us from beneath the dirt-bordered brown edge of his *veshti,* the traditional ankle-length garment, which had once been white and was now yellowing with age. We sat opposite him, straight-backed, watching as the voice emanated from his vulturelike body, with shoulders that stuck up higher than his cheekbones.

"Vidya, you aren't paying attention," he said, a worried look on his wizened face. "Malati has progressed to singing *varnams* already. You have so much to learn. If you don't pay attention, you won't even progress to the *geetham* stage, and what will they say to you when the boy's family comes to visit?"

I wanted to tell him that was just why I hated the music lesson: because it was for the future groom's benefit, so that when we were "seen" by his family, they could discuss our domestic talents—how well we sang, how low we kept our voices and eyes and heads when we weren't singing. I wanted to tell him I might even have liked his lesson if we were taught to please ourselves rather than to entertain and enhance the quality of men's lives when we became wives. But he chewed on the tip of his wispy white mustache so sadly that I swallowed my words and tried to sing for his sake.

After the lesson, I found Chinni chithi and told her I was to mind the baby.

"I'm sorry," Chinni chithi said. "I didn't want to make more work for you."

"This isn't work," I said emphatically. "Mangalam is a lovely baby. It'll be a pleasure to mind her."

Chinni chithi gave me a shy smile. "Thank you," she said.

I twirled my fingers in front of Mangalam's face and she gurgled at me. I picked her up and rocked her gently. Chinni chithi thanked me again as she scuttled off to the kitchen.

Within minutes, Mangalam was asleep in my arms. I was glad she slept so soundly, but it was boring watching her sleep. I wished I had brought my books with me. I missed books. If I could read while Mangalam slept, the hours would go a lot faster.

I picked up the baby again and walked out of the room. I stuck my head in the dining room and saw Malati, Sarasa chithi and periamma gossiping together. Avoiding them, I walked toward the front of the house and stood at the foot of the stairs, wondering if there was anything I could do other than walk to and fro the way I had already come.

Then I remembered that the house had a library. Appa had told me it was his favorite part of the house. I hadn't thought of it until now because I'd never seen it before—it was upstairs. I had never thought of trying to find it during the summers because I'd always brought a few books to read with me and by the time I was done with them, we were back in Bombay again. But now, it was different. I was here to stay and there was no way I could play outside. Books would help me escape the boundaries of the house, in my mind at least.

The staircase stood silent and empty. But it was forbidding. The barrier between the two floors of the house was unbroken except at mealtimes, when the men descended into our realm. Only men used the stairs. If anyone caught me walking up them, what would periamma do to me?

I put my foot on the first step hesitantly. I wondered if my heart was pounding loudly enough to wake the baby up. I clutched her tightly with one hand, picked up my long skirt with the other and climbed slowly.

At the top of the stairs, there was a door and a long corridor. The door probably led to the men's hall, so I walked the corridor. It was quiet.

At the end of the corridor, there was another choice. Two doors—one ornate and carved, of rosewood; the other more functional, of teak. I put my ear against the rosewood door. Silence. Silence also behind the other door. I bent as low as I could. The baby stirred. I stiffened, but she did not cry out. A quick look through the peephole showed me that the rosewood door led to a study. Thatha's study. I caught a glimpse of him sitting with his back to me at a rolltop desk, writing.

The teak door opened easily, revealing a room lined with

books. There were books of all sorts—worn paperbacks that looked as though they were at least a century old, leather-bound volumes embossed with gold letters on the spines: books on art, books on religion, books on history, poetry anthologies, atlases, novels.

I walked up and down the length of the room, gazing at the books with delight. The library was larger than I'd ever imagined. It must have taken decades just to get such a vast collection together. Did they all belong to thatha? Was he the one who had arranged them so neatly, categorizing them by subject?

A small wooden stepladder stood in the corner, yellow paint peeling off it. I wanted to climb it so I could read the titles that were on the top shelves, but I couldn't climb ladders with Mangalam in my arms.

There were two narrow windows in the far corner, through which sunlight slipped in stealthily, like a jaundiced thief. To the right was a large window with a window seat big enough for me to sit on, big enough for the baby to sleep on. Next time I'd bring pillows with me and make her a comfortable bed. Today she'd sleep on my lap. Hopefully.

A leather-bound book with gold lettering on the spine caught my eye. It was *Oliver Twist*. I remembered Kitta's remark and smiled. The old grandfather clock at the far end of the library ticked softly.

I pulled the book off the shelf and settled down on the window seat to read it until the last pink blush of sunlight had faded. It was like a dream, finding this place. I turned on the lamps and read until the clock chimed half past seven, reminding me that it was time to go down and serve the men dinner.

Chinni Chithi

$\mathcal{I}$ couldn't help beaming joyfully as I served the men that evening. Finding the library was the best thing that had happened since our arrival in Madras. I smiled at appa, but of course he didn't smile back.

Kitta kept darting questioning glances in my direction, but I couldn't share my wonderful discovery with him, not with periamma and periappa and everyone else well within earshot.

"School go well?" he managed to ask me.

"I found *Oliver Twist*," I said under my breath, hoping my cryptic words would make him guess that I had sneaked into the library. Perhaps he could try to meet me there so we could talk every now and then.

Kitta looked very confused.

Before I could say any more, periamma walked over to breathe down my neck and glare at Kitta. "Stop chattering with your brother," she said, boxing both my ears.

After we finished our meal, my mother and my three aunts

sat together rolling *pakku,* black pieces of betel nut, into betel leaves: the traditional post-dinner snack that was supposed to freshen the breath. Periamma chewed with her mouth open as she and Sarasa chithi began to pick on Chinni chithi.

"It was your duty to conceive again," Sarasa chithi was saying.

I had to look closely at Chinni chithi's midriff before I thought I noticed the slight bulge that her cleverly worn sari almost disguised. She had one older son, Mangalam was just a baby and here she was, pregnant already.

"Perhaps you will miscarry, having made it so evident that you wanted no more children," periamma said. "After all, naming a child Mangalam says clearly to the Almighty that you wanted to stop with her. No child born after her could ever be considered lucky."

"It was very wrong to want to stop with just two," Sarasa chithi said, looking pointedly at my mother. "It is our duty, after all, to have children."

I noticed a tear dangling at the tip of Chinni chithi's tiny nose, trembling as though it was too afraid to fall without periamma's permission. You're not a servant, I thought. You're their sister-in-law, just a few years younger, that's all. Tell them to leave you alone.

"By the way, girl," periamma said to me. "You'll be rinsing your cousins' clothes every day from now on. Chinni will go to her parents' home soon for her pregnancy, and she can't manage the clothes anymore."

I said nothing.

"Did you hear me?"

I gave her a curt nod.

Chinni chithi looked at me apologetically. I returned it with my most encouraging smile. Of all my aunts, Chinni chithi was the only one I cared to help, and I wanted to make sure she understood that I wasn't annoyed at her in any way.

After I swept the floor with the bundle of twigs that served as the broom, I scrubbed it, squatting on my haunches. Periamma kept us well occupied. I was thankful I wasn't her servant; it was bad enough being her niece.

My back, my thighs and my knees were aching when I finally straightened up. I could fall asleep at once, but I wasn't about to.

I hesitated, not wanting to enter the sleeping hall yet. The sounds of the radio broadcast seeped out from the small room downstairs where the men sat after supper, twiddling and twisting the tortured knobs on the radio until it wailed into life. I listened to the sound of static mingled with reports of the war. I caught the words "disturbance of the peace"—it was the British phrase to describe any kind of protest. I moved closer to the room.

Someone had been jailed, but I couldn't catch the name of

the person. I wondered which of our leaders had been imprisoned lately. It had been a while since I'd paid attention to the news.

Kitta's voice rose above the sound of the radio broadcast. He wasn't commenting on the "disturbance of the peace" or saying anything about our leaders; he was talking about the war instead.

"It's the World War all over again," I overheard him say. "Fighting is breaking out everywhere."

"No, no." That was periappa's voice. "What do you know about the Great War, boy? It was before your time. This war is different."

"I think Kitta has a point." I didn't recognize that voice. Chinni chithi's husband, perhaps? Most of the men never spoke to us when we served them.

I waited for a few minutes nervously, hoping to catch more of the conversation. Then I decided it wasn't worth the risk of getting caught eavesdropping on the men. I sneaked away quickly and noiselessly into the women's sleeping hall before the men could stream out and catch me lurking in the shadows.

Hans Brinker

Thus began my daily routine for the next two weeks: work, school, music, library, more work. And a half hour of standing in the shadows listening to snatches of news on the radio. They reported on the war that was always coming closer and involving more countries and the Indian freedom fighters who were always getting out of one prison and into another unless they were tortured or hung to death in between.

I only saw appa and Kitta at mealtimes, but Kitta could not say much, and appa's eyes never flickered with any sign of recognition.

The girls at school ignored me despite my best efforts to make friends. So I concentrated on my schoolwork instead. But though I excelled at every subject, Mrs. Rao continued to hate me.

The library was my only blessing. Every time I climbed the stairs, my heart lifted. All day, I looked forward to the happy hours I spent in that beautiful room. My guilt over appa's fate was too heavy to carry up there, and I learned to leave it below, somewhere on the ground floor. I left the house far behind as I walked on the path paved by the books, and every evening, baby Mangalam slept soundly on the bed I made for her on the window seat.

I tried to read every book I remembered seeing in appa's hands. I met people he had spoken of: Tagore, whose concept of freedom transcended all previous notions of the word; Sarojini Naidu, whose poetry sang and sparkled; Ramana Maharishi, whose profound philosophy I could not fully understand.

The evening after I finished Ramana Maharishi, I searched for something different—a light and easy read. It was a while since I'd read a good novel. My eyes fell on the green spine of a title that proclaimed *Hans Brinker and the Story of the Silver Skates*. I was intrigued. Silver skates? I pulled it off the shelf. It was too thick to be a fairy tale.

There was a dried-up insect on the cover. I blew it away gently and began to peruse the yellowing pages. The setting was the Netherlands, and there were descriptions of snow-covered earth. I settled into the window seat and started to read.

The story was about a boy called Hans and his younger sister, who lived together with their mother and a father who was like appa: a brave man who had been working to stop a dyke from flooding when his brain had been injured. I would not have remembered to go downstairs if the light had not dwindled, forcing me to stop reading.

The next day at school, I could hardly wait to return to the book. I even thought of sneaking it downstairs that evening. It took all my self-control not to run that risk. Hans and his sister were poor, and they were thinking of participating in a race where the victor would get a pair of silver skates—but that was only one thread in the story. One of the characters was a doctor, a crotchety but kind man. Would he help Hans's father?

The third day, when I finished the book, I felt I could hear temple bells chiming in my head. The doctor had operated on Hans's father, helping him return to normal. Hans hadn't won the race, but his father had won his memory back.

I put the book down and closed my eyes. I promised myself that I would wake appa up again. My actions had hurt him, but I could undo the damage. I would bring him back to normal so we could return to Bombay.

A Walk

The evening after I finished *Hans Brinker,* I waited beneath the forbidden staircase until Kitta came down, leading appa by the hand to take him on an evening walk. I knew I wasn't supposed to leave the house, but I stepped out with them, taking appa's other hand. Kitta looked surprised but pleased. We left the compound unnoticed. Fresh air flooded into my lungs, cool with relief.

"Kitta, I found the library," I said to him. "I go there every day."

"Don't get caught," he said warningly. Then his tone softened. "I'm glad you found it," he said. "You need something you like in this house."

"I love the library," I said. I told him all about the books I was reading. He nodded happily until I came to the part about Hans Brinker's father.

"That's just a story, Vidya," he said gently.

His lack of enthusiasm upset me. I turned my back to him and looked appa full in the face. "Appa, do you remember anything?" I asked. "Your name is Venkat. Do you know that? Do you know who Venkat is?"

"What do you think you are doing?" Kitta asked. He laid a hand on my shoulder. "Don't do this to yourself, Vidya."

"We've got to try and see how much he remembers, Kitta," I said determinedly. "Maybe he remembers something. Maybe we can jolt his memory somehow."

"You can't," Kitta said. He sounded resigned and hopeless. "It won't work."

I ignored him. "Venkat." I forced myself to address my father by his first name. "Venkat, can you hear me? Can you shake your head?"

The man who had been appa stared at the road with eyes that seemed blind. I tried again. "I'm your daughter. Vidya. This is Vidya," I said, pointing to myself. "Vidya." I took hold of appa's hands.

Kitta sighed. "Are you done? Vidya, can't you see he doesn't understand a thing? Leave him alone!"

"We can wake him up," I said doggedly. "We have to try."

"This is life, Vidya, not some silly story. Real life." Kitta pulled appa's hands out of mine. "Don't you think we haven't tried? We've all tried. Amma and I tried again and again those first few weeks. Our father is never going to be the same again, can't you see that? Never. Never. Never."

We glared at each other unblinkingly. Kitta was the first to break off. His back was hunched. The sight of his drooping shoulders shook something inside me.

Kitta began to walk away. Appa followed, as though he were a puppy. Kitta stopped and turned back. "Come, Vidya," he said softly. "Please."

I quickened my pace until we were together again. "Sorry," I said.

"I'm sorry too," Kitta said.

"How is college?" I asked, changing the subject. "Is Madras University any good?"

"Can't complain," he said briefly.

"Don't you want to talk to me?" I asked impatiently. "It's been ages since we talked."

"I think I've almost forgotten how to talk—I use my voice so little at home these days," he said.

I laughed. "I miss you," I said. "Can't you come to meet me in the library sometime?"

"I will," he promised. "I'll do my best. It's just that I'm busy, looking after appa as soon as I get back in the evenings."

"Who takes care of appa when you're away at college?" I asked.

"I leave him downstairs with amma," he said.

"Downstairs? With the women?" I asked, surprised.

"As periappa always reminds me, appa isn't a real man anymore, just an idiot," Kitta said dryly.

"How can you let periappa say that?" I asked. "Don't you ever want to punch him in the face?"

"I try not to think about what he says," Kitta replied.

"There are a lot of others in the world, saying far more important things. I try to concentrate on what's happening outside this house."

"Good for you," I said. "I don't even get to really read the newspaper every day, thanks to our dear aunt."

"I'm sorry," he said. "I know it's a lot worse for you. Boys have it better in this house, that's for sure."

I felt a strange tightness in my chest. I wanted to apologize for bringing him to this house, to confess that I was responsible for what had happened to appa, but I couldn't find the words.

"So how do you like school?" he continued. "Have you made any friends?"

"Friends? They're all like Malati, Kitta. The only thing they have on their minds is marriage."

"Maybe I should talk to them, then," he teased. "Are any of them pretty?"

I laughed again. It was good to be able to speak to him. He could always make me laugh.

We turned the corner of the road and the house came into view. Kitta stopped walking and looked at me for a moment. "Vidya, is there anything on your mind? You seem different these days."

I struggled for words. There was so much I was worried about. Marriage, most of all. Were periappa and periamma trying to marry me off so they could rid themselves of the idiot's daughter?

"Kitta, my horoscope. Are they circulating it? Do you know?" An icy shiver cut through me. "I don't want to get married, Kitta. I want to finish school." I stopped myself from saying anything about college. Kitta had enough to think of without adding that. But maybe he could at least help keep marriage at bay for a while.

Kitta didn't reply right away. "I'll do everything I can to make sure you aren't married off until you finish sixth form, okay?"

"Promise?"

"I'll do what I can. And don't worry. I'm the man of the house now, and they can't marry you off without my consent—I won't let them, I promise you that much."

He didn't sound terribly convincing.

It was still something, I told myself. More than I deserved, maybe, after all I had done to kill appa's soul.

We walked back together in silence. As the gate of the house creaked open, amma stepped out onto the verandah. "What are you doing, kanna?"

"We just went for a walk around the neighborhood," I answered.

"Kitta, promise me you'll never do this again." Her voice was shaking. "Please, Kitta. Please."

"It's not like we did anything wrong," I interrupted.

"You must be careful for your sister's sake, Kitta. Her prospects." Amma's hand was shaking too. "We're not on our own anymore. People will talk."

"Okay," Kitta said, releasing appa's hand to take hers for a moment. "Okay. I promise. Don't worry, amma."

I stalked back indoors, holding my head high.

Saraswathi Poojai

The next morning, Navarathri, the ten-day festival celebrating the victory of Goddess Durga over the bull-headed demon Mahisha, began. I remembered how we had celebrated the festival in Bombay. Appa had always set up the special staircase altar and Rifka had come over, as far back as I could remember, to help us decorate the altar with our Navarathri dolls.

"I'm going to arrange our Navarathri dolls," Malati said that evening after school. "Don't even think you can touch them."

"Go right ahead," I said. "I have better things to do."

As I walked away, periamma cast a suspicious glance in my direction. "Where are you going, girl?" she asked. Before I could answer, Malati distracted her, whining about my rudeness.

I walked away quickly before periamma could ask me more, snatching up Mangalam and nearly running upstairs in my haste to get to the library safely. I wandered up and down past the shelves, wondering what I was in a mood for. My eyes fell on a slim, navy blue volume of poetry with silver lettering on its spine. Within minutes, I had discovered Wordsworth and journeyed with him to hills and valleys in the British Isles. By the time I returned downstairs, I knew a verse from a poem by heart, "I wandered lonely as a cloud/that floats on high o'er vales and hills/when all at once I saw a crowd,/a host of golden daffodils . . . " I spent a lot of time that evening wondering what daffodils were shaped like.

All week long, women from the neighborhood came to the house to sing and share sweetmeats. I got to clean up after the visitors left.

On Saraswathi poojai, the ninth day of Navarathri, I decided to sneak the *Hans Brinker* book down from the library. Saraswathi poojai was my favorite festival, a day dedicated to the spinster goddess of learning, when we worshipped books. I hid *Hans Brinker* in my pile of schoolbooks in the poojai room, where everyone else had stacked their favorite books. As I stood beneath the sandalwood carving of Goddess Saraswathi riding a white swan, her long, delicate fingers caressing the strings of her *veena,* I prayed as never before. Fervently. Devoutly. For so long that periamma finally made amma come in and touch me gently on the shoulder to remind me that I should leave the room.

"Please, please, let them forget to marry me off to some stupid man," I said to the goddess. "Give me the chance to study, to learn, to go to college. You showed me the way to the library. Please show me how to stay single like you."

Then something happened that made my thoughts stray far from spinsterhood.

❦

Periamma confronted me in the kitchen at dinnertime that night as I was balancing the water pot against my waist, getting ready to pour water into the men's tumblers. "Where do you go after you return from school? I never see you."

"I mind the baby," I said. "You told me to, remember?"

"Where do you go with the baby?" she asked accusingly.

"I don't go anywhere. I stay in this house," I said.

"Where in this house?"

"In this house," I repeated.

"I asked you where," she repeated threateningly. "Answer me. Or are you like your idiot father now? Incapable of comprehension?"

Sarasa chithi tittered. Chinni chithi said nothing, just stared down at her feet and wiggled her silver toe rings. Amma looked fixedly at the pot she was stirring on the stove. It was as if she had not heard, except she must have because periamma's voice was always loud.

Periamma held up the copy of *Hans Brinker*. "Where did you get this?" she demanded. "What's this doing in your pile of schoolbooks?"

"I go to the library," I said, staring straight back into her eyes unblinkingly. "Upstairs."

"You shouldn't," she said, as though that decided it. But I was not going to let it end that way. I was tired of letting her overrule me.

"Who says I shouldn't?" I asked. "You? Periappa? Thatha? Is there a rule that I can't?"

"Thatha," she said firmly.

"Really? He's never told me that himself. I'm going to ask him."

Chinni chithi was still gazing at her feet. Her toes squirmed like frightened worms. Amma looked up with worried eyes.

I marched out of the kitchen and stood in front of thatha, who was sitting quietly in the dining room, looking down at his plate. In my entire life, I had never said anything to him before directly, ever. Just brought him buttermilk or more rice or whatever it was he said he needed.

"Thatha, do you want any more food?"

"No," he said absently, not looking up. He hardly cared who served him. It was a wonder he recognized me at all.

"May I use the library upstairs?" I couldn't hide the slight tremor in my voice. It was unusually high-pitched.

Malati gasped. I ignored her.

"What?" Thatha looked up, his hand halfway to his mouth, a muddy rivulet of sambhar dripping from his palm.

"What?" he repeated, sitting up very straight and glancing at me from under his bushy gray eyebrows.

"I want to go to the library every evening after school," I said clearly. "I don't shirk from my work. I take my baby cousin, Mangalam, and look after her. I just want to study, to read while I mind her. That's all."

Somehow every man who was still sitting at his plate had heard what I'd said.

Periappa was, of course, the first to object. "What sort of nonsense is that? Girls shouldn't go upstairs."

Before I could reply, a boy a few years older than Kitta, whom I had never seen before, cut in softly, "Why not?"

I waited to hear periappa bellow at the boy like a buffalo, but he didn't. What power did the boy have? He was probably related to appa's sister, my aunt, who lived in Coimbatore. A relative from the groom's side of the family, whom everyone had to treat respectfully so that my aunt would be treated well in their home.

"I don't see why she can't read while she's minding her baby cousin," the boy continued, his tone firm.

I noticed how handsome the boy was. I could tell that he was tall, though he was sitting cross-legged on the floor. He looked manlier than Kitta, with broad shoulders, muscular arms and thick, curly, blue-black hair. His large eyes seemed to pierce through periappa. Periappa wriggled uncomfortably, the folds of his stomach jiggling as he shifted position.

Kitta joined in. "Vivekanandha talked about respecting women and raising them to the equal status they had during Vedic times, but we just don't bother to do it," he said, looking straight into thatha's eyes.

I'd never heard of Vivekanandha before. If I ever was allowed into the library again, I promised myself I would look for Vivekanandha's books.

Thatha spoke. "Why do you want to go upstairs?"

"To read, of course. She told us that already," the boy said before I could reply. "Why else would anyone want to go to the library?"

"She has my permission," thatha said slowly and clearly, looking at periappa. "A love of books is not an evil thing."

Kitta and the boy exchanged triumphant smiles. Periappa shook his head solemnly, as though a great evil had descended upon the house. But thatha didn't care to dwell on the subject any longer. He just went off to wash his hands. That was the end of the matter as far as he was concerned.

I walked into the kitchen and spun around once, twice, three times, twirling my hands in the air. Periamma grunted like an angry sow. Amma walked toward me and touched my cheek gently. She was smiling too. When periamma turned her back, Chinni chithi looked at me, and I saw the corner of her lip curl up in a quick smile. I threw my arm around my mother's shoulders and gave Chinni chithi's hand a gentle squeeze. I felt ecstatic.

When I reentered the dining room, Kitta glanced up cautiously and mouthed, "Congratulations." I smiled.

Out of habit, I looked briefly into appa's face. His glazed eyes told me he had understood nothing.

Raman

Over the next two weeks, I discovered *Ivanhoe,* a novel by
Sir Walter Scott, filled with endless and evocative descriptions.
The story was romantic, and it fit my mood—Ivanhoe was a
chivalrous hero who gallantly defended beautiful women.

I also looked forward to serving the men at mealtimes because that was when I could see the boy again. He glanced at
me every now and then, and when we were sure no one else
was looking, we risked exchanging a quick smile. But October
was over before I finally got to speak to him face-to-face.

That chance came in early November, the morning of the
first day of Deepavali, the most important Hindu festival of
light. I was picking flowers for the morning poojai. In north-
ern India, people said the festival celebrated the return of
the just King Rama to his lands after fourteen years of exile;
in southern India, we said it celebrated the victory of Lord
Krishna over the demon Narakasura, but appa had explained
to me that the true meaning of the festival was far deeper—it
was a celebration of the spiritual light, which glowed within

every human being. My flower basket was bright with yellow chrysanthemums and red hibiscus, and I turned my attention to the patch of aromatic herbs, *maru* and *dhavanam*. Their fragrance was faint on the air.

I had a sudden impulse to breathe in their scent. Mere mortals were not supposed to stick their noses into bouquets that were offered to the gods, but I couldn't help flouting the holy rule.

As I let the fragrance fill my lungs, I felt someone's eyes on the back of my neck. I turned. The boy was standing there.

"I'm Raman," he said. "Your father's sister's husband's brother."

What are you doing here? I thought. Maybe my eyes gave me away. He answered as though I had voiced my thoughts aloud. "My family lives in Coimbatore, but I go to college in Madras. The university where your brother studies now."

He had seen me burying my nose in the flowers. How could he not have? I could feel my cheeks flushing with embarrassment, and I made a move as though to toss the flowers away.

"I don't think God would mind if you enjoyed His flowers," he said.

I flashed my best smile at him. "God is not a man," I said.

"Yes and no," he countered. "The Supreme Being is the one and the many. Male and female. Formless and yet with form. Whosoever the devotee, and whatsoever the form that is worshipped, know that I am worshipped."

"The *Bhagavad Gita*," I said to show that I knew what he was quoting.

"You've read the *Gita*?" He sounded surprised. He paused and then asked, "You want to add some *ixora* to your basket?"

Without waiting for an answer, he reached up and plucked a bunch of pink flowers that were too high for me to reach and dropped them in my basket. He was taller even than appa.

"Thank you," I said. "Raman anna." Adding that word, *anna*, older brother, a term of respect. I didn't like the sound of it. It appeared he didn't like it either.

"Please just call me Raman," he said.

"Do you like it in this house, Raman?"

"It's good of them to keep me," he said.

They have to, I thought. You're a relative from the groom's side of the family.

"Yes, they have to keep me, don't they?" Again, my unspoken words had spilled out through my eyes—they were sometimes a little too eloquent for my liking. "But I can't say anything negative about my treatment here." He quoted a Tamil proverb, "Never speak badly about a household that has served you a salted meal."

"It depends on how much food they serve you," I said. "I can't think kindly of a house in which I'm hungry after every meal, even if the food is salted."

"It can't have been easy to move here so suddenly," he

said gently. "And your father's illness must be difficult for you too."

I swallowed. His tone made me want to share more about my life in Bombay, but I was afraid it would make me break down. I changed the topic.

"So how come you weren't in the house when we arrived?" I asked. "We came here some weeks before the Navarathri festival. And we used to come every summer. I never noticed you before."

"I noticed you some time ago," he said, looking straight into my eyes.

I felt myself blushing.

"You never saw me before because I go back to Coimbatore over the summer holidays," he continued. "And it sounds like this year you arrived in late September, just around the time I came down with typhoid. I had to stay upstairs, quarantined, in a little room by myself, for about five weeks."

"Who brought you your food?" I asked.

"The only Brahmin servant in the house—the cook," he said.

"I wonder what her name is," I said absently.

"Who?" he asked.

"The cook," I said. "In this house, the servants have no names. In Bombay, we knew them. Here periamma makes me rinse vessels after the maid washes them to get rid of her polluting non-Brahmin touch. I even have to rinse the clothes again after the maid washes them before I can bring them back into the house."

"Do you miss Bombay?" he asked. "Sorry, it was a stupid question. Of course you must."

"It wasn't a stupid question," I said. I found myself telling him about Walsingham Girls' School and how different the teachers and students had been there. About Rifka. And my other friends. About the house and the sparkling waters of Mahim beach. And Raja and how much I missed his quiet, unwavering love for me. But nothing about the march or about appa. Still, it was more than I had spoken in months.

I was sorry when my basket was full and I had to walk back to the house.

"Why are you smiling?" periamma said suspiciously as I came into the poojai room with the full basket.

"Because it is Deepavali," I said. "And I am thinking of the inexhaustible light inside me. *Aham amrithe, amritham bramhani*, I am immortal because the light of God is within me, the Vedas say."

She looked a bit bewildered for a moment, trying to tell if I was being pious, in which case it would be wrong of her to box my ears (especially in the prayer room), or if I was being impudent. I left before she could make up her mind.

I sneaked up to the library and scrounged about until I

found a pen and an old sheet of letter paper. At last I had something positive to tell Rifka.

Dear Rifka,

Sorry I was so abrupt before I left; I just couldn't talk about what was happening. It was all too much. Thanks for understanding.

Appa is still unwell, and he's never going to get any better.

I paused and stuck my pen in my mouth. I didn't want to tell her everything about appa yet.

Living here is, well, what you'd expect, based on everything I've told you about our summer visits. I'm glad we Hindus have a festival at least once a month or I'd never really speak to Kitta. Amma made sure I could go to school, but I haven't made any friends there yet, and they don't play any sports.

I reread my sentences. I didn't want to sound self-pitying. Besides, I'd wanted to write the letter for a whole other reason that I hadn't even mentioned yet. I continued.

But anyway, I wanted to write today because I finally did make a friend. And you'd never guess this—but he's a boy!

He's really tall, taller than appa, and he must be a few years older than Kitta. His name is Raman.

I filled up an entire page with details about how I met Raman and about the library and finished by sending my regards to her family. Then I sealed it, took it downstairs and put it away carefully in my schoolbag, wondering where I'd get the money to buy a stamp.

Later that morning, on my way to school, I had an idea. I got off two stops earlier than normal and walked to the post office. I used the money I had saved on the bus fare to buy a stamp for the letter. I felt an excited lurch in the pit of my stomach as I opened the red postbox and slid the envelope into it. It landed inside with a joyful clang, as though it was celebrating my small secret victory over periamma. I couldn't help grinning all day at school. Before I left, I even wished Mrs. Rao a happy Deepavali.

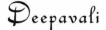

Deepavali

The first evening of Deepavali was festive, and even we, the children of the idiot, were allowed to play with firecrackers. The man who had been my father—would he be frightened now by all the noise? I cast an anxious look in his direction, but he seemed to be watching the fireworks without fear. It was comforting somehow to see his solid body outlined against the darkening sky—looking calm and quiet—like a mountain. I could almost believe he was completely there.

"Don't worry," amma said. "He's all right."

I nodded. Then I surprised myself by asking, "Are you all right too, amma?"

"Yes, kanna," she said to me, the term of endearment slipping out of her lips nervously.

I closed my eyes for a moment and all the others vanished—it was just appa, amma, Kitta and me, watching the Vishnu *chakrams*, wheels of sparkling fire, whirling like Lord Vishnu's discus across the slightly uneven ground before the front steps of our home. Amma had looked particularly pretty on Deepavali nights, her eyes sparkling with light, brighter than all the fireworks on earth, smiling up at appa. I remembered how my parents used to look at each other—a special gaze they reserved for no one else.

"Amma, you look beautiful this evening," I said.

She swallowed and touched my cheek with her finger, but before she could get too sentimental, I plunged the *mathappu* that I was holding into a candle flame. I held the sparkler in my hands as it sizzled and spurted, shooting out hot jets of light until it fizzled out.

"Be careful, Vidya," amma said.

"Yes, yes. Don't worry," I replied.

We were all out in front of the house, admiring the fiery fountains leaping from the conical *busvanam* fireworks. I took a few steps back and reached into the box of sparklers again, my eyes still fixed on the dancing lights. My hand brushed accidentally against someone else's. It was Raman's. I drew back, startled.

Raman flushed with embarrassment. "Sorry. I wasn't looking," he said awkwardly. But he did not sound apologetic.

The tips of my fingers were tingling. I turned away to hide my confusion.

"I wasn't paying attention," he mumbled, quickly taking a few large steps back, putting the requisite distance between us.

Kitta was acting silly, lighting bombs that made loud noises, while Chinni chithi brought out the sweets. Since thatha was around, I could have my fill. I snatched up the biggest *badhusha* I could see, licking off the pistachio nuts on top and savoring every bite of its sugary dough. For once, I would go to bed with a satisfied stomach.

I dreamed of Raman that night. We were standing in a park, drenched in sunshine. He was reaching for my hand. The distance between us grew at first, so we couldn't touch. My hand was like lead. I was unable to lift it. At last, my hand came unstuck from my body and our fingers interlocked.

I awoke, shocked at the impropriety of my thoughts. How could I dream of holding a man's hand? Someone I hardly knew?

I said a silent prayer of thankfulness that neither periamma nor my other two aunts could see my dreams, and I lay awake for hours, scared to sleep, afraid of the uncontrollable wanderings of my own mind.

Raman's Gift

On the morning of the second day of Deepavali, periamma, Malati and Sarasa chithi began chattering before dawn about the new silk saris they had been given for the festival. Chinni chithi didn't join their boasting. But after we had all bathed, she pulled out a sari box, and throwing an apologetic glance in our direction, she followed the other women into the poojai room, where they would consecrate their Deepavali saris before wearing them. Appa had always taken us to the store and bought us new silks to wear for the morning of the second day of the festival, but this year we had none.

Amma put her arm around me. "I'm sorry," she began, but I cut her off.

"You shouldn't be," I said. "I have more saris than I need, amma. Anyway, Deepavali is about the inner light, not about wearing new clothes."

She smiled at me gratefully. "We should still say a prayer," she suggested. I nodded.

The other women were leaving the poojai room as amma

and I walked toward it. I heard a man clear his throat behind me and looked back, surprised. It was thatha.

I stared at him, puzzled. What was he doing downstairs so early?

"For you to wear for this morning," he said gruffly, thrusting a box into my hands. The box said *Nalli* on the outside. Nalli was the most famous sari shop in all of southern India. Then he shoved another box into my hands. "For your mother," he said, and left as I stuttered my thanks.

Amma smiled the widest smile I had seen in a long, long time.

"Go on, open it," she said as I traced over the letters of the shop's name with my fingers. I untied the strings that held my sari box together. Thatha had given me a gorgeous pink Kanchipuram silk, embroidered liberally with gold thread. Amma's was simpler, but it was also a fine silk. Amma set the saris in front of the altar, closed her eyes and murmured a prayer.

Malati watched angrily as I changed into my new attire.

"Where did you get that?" she demanded.

"Thatha gave it to me," I replied.

"It looks cheap," Malati said cattily.

"It's a Nalli silk," I said, unable to keep the note of triumph out of my voice. "From Kanchipuram."

"It's ugly, regardless where it's from," she huffed, but her eyes bulged with jealousy.

The sari was thick and fell in perfect folds to my feet. The heavy pleats swished pleasantly as I walked up and down the room in front of amma.

"I can't believe thatha gave me this," I said.

"You look beautiful. That color suits you perfectly," amma said, her eyes bright. "But he really shouldn't have given *me* anything."

"Nonsense. You deserve that and more," I said as she changed into it.

Amma's words reminded me that I hadn't seen my own reflection for a long time. I wanted to see how the sari looked on me. Perhaps I had grown pretty? All I was allowed in the mornings was a quick peep into the polished surface of a plate so I could place the pottu in the right place and make sure the red dot was round. With periamma quacking, "Quick, quick, quick," the whole time, like an old goose.

I wanted to look at my entire body. There was a full-length mirror in one corner of the library—one that I hadn't ever had the courage to use. Until now.

My heart was pounding as I climbed the stairs early that morning, dressed in my new sari, hoping no one would notice. I walked over to the long mirror recessed between two bookshelves.

My body had changed. I stared at the thickness of my brows, the sure straightness with which they dared to grow out on either side of my broad bridge of nose. I had inherited my eyebrows from my father—as I looked at the unbending line that they drew across my face, my heart lurched.

I shook my head and forced myself to look at the mirror again and see me, just me, nothing beyond me. I had lost some weight. No surprise there. Bones were jutting out at strange angles. I squared my shoulders and looked at myself sideways.

Beauty had never mattered much to me before, but now I gazed at my reflection critically. I looked nothing like Malati, but was it possible that I was attractive too, at least when I was dressed up? Did Raman find me pretty at all?

I was pulling at my earlobes, wishing they would curve out like Malati's perfect crescents, when I caught the reflection of a stealthy movement behind me. I froze with fear. That was that. I had been caught preening myself in front of my own reflection. I would be banished from the library forever.

I turned slowly around to face the intruder. Raman was gazing at me. I blushed. How long had he been watching?

To my surprise, he looked just as embarrassed as I did.

"Sorry," he said. He was holding something in his hands. He thrust it into mine. "This is for you."

It was an empty notebook.

"An empty book?"

"You can write anything you want in it. It might help."

He turned on his heel and strode swiftly away before I could thank him. I sat on the window seat and picked up *The*

Mayor of Castorbridge, a Thomas Hardy novel I had started to read. His prose was like poetry, and I loved the way his words flowed, but for the first time, they could not carry me away. I didn't even make it down one page. *Pusthakam hastha bushanam,* my book is just an ornament for my hands today, I thought, slapping it shut.

I took a pen from the writing desk and opened Raman's gift. I began with the day of our arrival in the house at the end of September, describing in as much detail as I could the time that had passed since then. I allowed a flood of unspoken sentences to spill onto the white paper, splashing it with blue streaks, like summer sky piercing through a white wall of cloud. I spoke of the world that seemed to have suddenly opened itself to me after I had met Raman. I ended by describing the library—how beautiful it looked to me that day and every day. If someone had asked me then what human invention I valued most, I would have told them without hesitation that it was the written word.

The Library

The next day, on the way to school, I decided to get off the bus one stop early and walk the rest of the way. It felt good to walk alone for that short distance, unsupervised and free for at least a few minutes. In the evening, I caught the bus one stop closer to home, rejoicing all the way that Malati was no longer going to school with me.

During my music lesson with Malati, I thought about the change I had saved on the bus fare by riding a shorter distance. Was it stealing if I holed money away every day from now on by walking an extra stop? I decided it wasn't.

When I took baby Mangalam up to the library to mind her, I put the paise I had saved into a sequined drawstring pouch that appa had given me long ago and hid it behind the fat volume of Scott's *Ivanhoe* along with my diary. It was a strange security, knowing I had money of my own. Money with which I could do anything I wanted to. I could never save enough for college, but at least I could buy a few more stamps. And if I was ever allowed out of the house long enough—maybe a small present for amma someday.

I counted my coins, feeling like Silas Marner, a miser whose only joy in life came from counting his stash of gold coins. He was the hero in the book I was reading, written by a woman who had assumed a masculine pen name. She'd had to disguise her gender so her novels could get published.

I had just stuck the pouch back in its hiding place when the door of the library opened and Raman walked in.

At once, I started writing furiously in my diary. Raman pretended he was searching for a reference of some sort and then sat down at the writing desk near my window seat.

The next day, Raman provided no excuse for why he was in the library again. I had been attempting to read *Pride and Prejudice,* by Jane Austen. I put the book away as soon as he came in after deciding to avoid her work in the future—her world seemed filled with marriages.

The day after that, my heart skipped like a stone across water as I climbed the stairs to the library. Raman was already there when I arrived, sitting at the writing desk, studying.

We talked for a while, and then I settled into the window seat and began to write in my book. A few minutes later, the sound of a heavy footfall broke the companionable silence that stretched between us.

Thatha walked in and started scanning the shelves.

What was he doing here? Could he hear us in his study?

Did he know that we were spending time together alone and unchaperoned? I shrank back in the window seat, hoping he wouldn't notice my presence.

Raman did just the opposite. "Are you searching for a book?" he asked thatha. "May I help you find something?"

"Yes, perhaps you could help. Have you seen my copy of Bharathiyar's *Kuyil Pattu*?"

Raman stood up, unperturbed. "I think I might have," he said, rising and pulling a book off the shelf to my left. "Here it is."

"Ah," said thatha, unmistakably pleased. "Read it, have you?"

"Yes," Raman said simply. I stared intently at my knees while Raman and thatha conversed at length about Bharathiyar's imagery. When I dared to look up, thatha's gaze met mine and the ends of his mouth twitched. In the deepening twilight, I couldn't tell if he was amused or annoyed.

After thatha left, Raman looked very pleased with himself. "What's the matter with you?" he asked. "You look like a nervous squirrel."

"I think thatha was checking up on us," I said.

"I'm sure he was," Raman said, grinning down at me. "So what?"

"I'm not sure I like it," I said. "Appa always trusted me."

"Don't be silly," Raman said dismissively. "It's for your own protection. He has to look after you—you're an unmarried girl."

"Don't you care how much trouble we could have been in?" I asked.

"I care a lot about—about—" He broke off and fidgeted uneasily for a moment. Then he tried again. "I care a lot about my friends," he said.

We looked at each other. The sky had darkened into an inky black, but we did not turn on the lights.

Then the clock struck half past seven, and I leaped off the window seat, flustered. Raman turned the lights on and I hurried downstairs to serve supper.

I barely looked at Raman as I served him that evening. I felt strangely shy.

That night, I lay awake a long time looking out at the stars in the patch of sky framed by the window. It struck me that one floor above, Raman might just be looking at the same spot. It gave me a pleasant shiver to think of the possibility, that we could share a moment together even when we were apart.

The Outhouse

Nine days after Deepavali, I was sent to the outhouse, banished from society because I had my period. It was another one of the house rules that I hated—a woman with her period was considered too unclean to be seen. Her presence and touch were polluting, and she had to spend three days imprisoned in an airless room that reeked because it was so close to the toilets.

My meals were left outside on the ground for me as though I were a dog. I had to pick them up without being seen. I could not change my clothes or bathe either because I was too dirty to be allowed into the bathing rooms. For three days, I had nothing to do but think of how stupid this custom was and wait for my bleeding to stop. I spent hours staring at the banana tree outside the barred slit that served as the window.

When I could finally bathe and reenter the house, the feeling of humiliation still burned inside me. At school that day, I had a difficult time keeping my mind on the lessons.

That evening, in the library, I searched for a book by

Vivekanandha. I wanted to listen to the words of a man who had truly respected women, who truly believed in human equality. Vivekanandha lamented that Hindus had allowed their wonderfully spiritual religion to descend and become fettered by ritual. He even said he sometimes felt closer to God on the football field than he did inside a temple.

I slapped the book shut, feeling agitated. Why did no one listen to his words? Why didn't Hindus pay any real attention to their own philosophers?

My thoughts were rudely disturbed by Raman, who confronted me with a worried frown. "So, where were you these past days?" he demanded possessively. "I've been wondering what happened."

I felt a warm flush on my neck, although I knew I had nothing to feel ashamed of. "I was away," I said euphemistically, not meeting his gaze.

His eyebrows knitted together quizzically.

The irritation I had been trying to suppress surged back through me. "I was out," I repeated.

"Oh, that," Raman said, suddenly catching on and looking terribly embarrassed. "Sometimes I wish I were a woman. How nice to have three days off from work every month, three days to just sit and be lazy."

I stared at him, shocked. "Lazy? Is that what you think?" I shook my head. "Do you even know what the outhouse is like?

Have you ever been told that your touch is polluting? Do you have any idea what it feels like when someone leaves your plate on the floor for you like you're a dog? I didn't even treat Raja so disrespectfully."

"Sorry," he mumbled, and then added, "at least it's only a few days."

"Even a few days of solitary confinement is wrong," I hissed. "Shunning women and shutting them up is unjustifiable." I couldn't control the annoyance that was bubbling inside me.

"I agree." Raman's voice was unusually high-pitched. "I think it's a ridiculous custom."

"Men never have to talk about their bodies," I said. My anger was rising like floodwaters about to burst a dam. "What gives everyone the right to intrude on a woman's privacy?"

"You're right. I never thought about it before . . ." His voice trailed off. He looked very uncomfortable.

"I'm sick of you thoughtless men," I snapped. "Sometimes I wish I could send you all away."

He asked nervously, "So you could live in a world with just women?"

"Yes," I said shortly, trying to regain my composure. I realized that I was railing about every injustice that had been meted to us in this house, not just the experience of the past few days, and that none of it was Raman's fault. I struggled to stop.

Raman nodded a few times. Then a wicked smile turned up the corner of his mouth. "All women?" he asked. "Even Malati?"

I had to laugh, but a pang of jealousy shot through me. Did Raman think Malati was pretty?

Raman joined in my laughter, and I felt my anger ebb away slowly.

"So can I read what you've been writing in that book I gave you?" he asked after a pause.

I shook my head. "It's mine now, isn't it?"

He grinned. "I was joking. I respect your privacy. Truly. And I respect you."

I blushed.

"So what have you been reading lately?" he asked.

"I'm between books," I told him. "Do you have a recommendation?"

The awkwardness between us dissolved like dust in the air being washed away by a monsoon downpour. And once again, the minutes ticked away all too quickly before I was forced to return downstairs.

Karthigai

$\mathcal{F}$ive days after my emergence from the outhouse, on the first full moon day after Deepavali, it was time for Karthigai, the second festival of light.

The late afternoon was damp and a velvety curtain of cloud shaded the sun, like a sari drawn across the face of a woman. After I returned from school, periamma confronted me.

"Here," she said, thrusting an opened envelope into my hands. "A letter for you."

"You read it?" I asked, shocked.

"Of course," Malati chimed in. "Of course we read it. It arrived this morning."

"It was addressed to *me*," I said, annoyed.

Malati snorted.

"You're an unmarried girl," periamma said. "You cannot receive letters unless they've been read first by an older person. Where did you get a stamp to write to her in the first place?"

"I brought stamps with me from Bombay so I could write to my friends," I said, tightening my grasp on my letter. "Kitta posted it for me." The lie rolled off my tongue easily. It was not a lie, I told myself, it was a form of self-defense.

"You're not to send anyone a letter unless I read it first, understand?"

I bit back my irritated words, cluching my letter so tightly that my nails pierced my palms.

I turned and walked away to find baby Mangalam. She was awake, and she reached out for me with her tiny hands, smiling. "Did you have a good day at school?" Chinni chithi asked.

"Yes," I said, doing my best to sound cheerful. "Yes, it was nice."

"Sarasa is minding Mangalam today," Chinni chithi said, lifting the baby. Before I could register my surprise at the unusual arrangement, amma entered. There were dark circles under her eyes, but they brightened when they met mine. Then she noticed the letter I had almost crushed and looked apologetic.

"I'm sorry about the letter, Vidya," she said. "Thatha was handing it to me, but periamma tore it out of my hand later and opened it. I tried—"

I interrupted. "It doesn't matter. At least periamma gave it to me."

"It's from Rifka, isn't it?"

I nodded.

"Let me know if you need money for a stamp to reply to her," amma said, lowering her voice.

I smiled and nodded again. "Thanks," I said.

I sat down in a corner of the room and smoothed out the letter as best I could.

Dearest Vidya,

I was thrilled to hear from you at last. I would have been happier, of course, if it had been filled with good news. When I opened it, I was so excited—somehow I was sure that you were writing to say everything was fine again and that you'd be returning to Bombay. Silly me. I guess I dream a lot—too much, probably.

I miss you terribly. The other girls at school do too. Mrs. Batlivala says we lost the best student. She never told you she thought you were the best student when you were here, did she? I could tell she really meant it.

We just lost a volleyball match yesterday, and I'm sure we'd have won it if you were still on our team. I can't believe you don't have any sports at your new school—that's awful. I also can't believe you haven't made any friends yet—that just doesn't sound like you. Those girls must be really odd. Poor you.

I'm glad you sounded so cheerful in spite of everything. It can't be easy for any of you. How is Kitta? Is he enjoying col-

lege? You haven't said too much about your family, just that your dad is still unwell. That must be so difficult for your mother especially. I wish we could do something.

Is there any chance you can come here to visit us? Maybe for at least a part of the summer holiday? My parents said they'd be glad to pay for your train ticket, and we have more than enough room for all of you—you know that, don't you? My parents ask to send their regards to all of you. Even my brother asked about you the other day.

Good luck with everything. I reread some parts of your letter with lots of smiles, and I have lots of questions that I won't ask just yet. Maybe you know what they are and you'll answer them next time you write.

Waiting to hear from you again.

Lots of love and best wishes,

Rifka

I exhaled with relief. Dear old Rifka. She'd had enough sense not to mention the complaints I'd made about periamma and Malati and Sarasa chithi. She hadn't written a word about Raman either. Thank goodness she was so perceptive. I read the letter again three times, savoring the sound of her words in my head, before I tucked it away into my schoolbag.

Amma was standing there when I looked up. "How's Rifka?" she asked as her face lightened.

"She's doing well," I said. "She sends her regards. So do her parents." I didn't mention that Rifka had invited us to visit. I knew amma didn't have enough money to pay for tickets to Bombay, and she'd never allow Rifka's parents to pay either.

Chinni chithi returned to the room, looking joyful. "Now we can decorate the house with Karthigai lamps, the three of us," she said. "That's why you aren't minding Mangalam today."

I smiled at her happily. The men would actually be allowed to mingle with us this evening as it was a festive day. Besides, less time inside the house with periamma and Malati and Sarasa chithi was always welcome.

I changed out of my school uniform and followed amma and Chinni chithi out. Amma poured oil into a small clay lamp carefully, without spilling a drop.

Chinni chithi clapped. I could tell she was delighted to be able to spend time doing something pleasant for a change and with just me and amma.

My eyes fell on her protruding belly, and she noticed it and smiled.

"I'll be leaving for my mother's house tomorrow," she said. I knew it was the custom for pregnant women to leave for their parents' homes when they were a few months pregnant. It was the only time they were allowed an extended visit with their own families.

"You must be looking forward to it," I said, taking a lamp from amma and placing it along the edge of the verandah.

"Yes, very much," she said. Her face glowed. "And I'll take Mangalam, so there will be one less chore for you to do," she continued.

"Oh!" The strangled exclamation escaped my lips before I could smother it. How would I be able to justify visiting the library if I didn't have the baby as an excuse?

Chinni chithi raised her eyebrows in surprise. "Is something wrong?"

I tried to cover up my gasp of fear. "No. It's just that I'll miss her." That was true, at least.

Chinni chithi smiled. "I know Mangalam will miss you too. She waits for you every evening, and her face lights up when you come to take her—have you noticed?"

I nodded, but my thoughts were elsewhere. Periamma would undoubtedly deny me permission to go to the library as soon as Mangalam was gone. I had to ask thatha about it the first opportunity I had.

I didn't have to wait long. Thatha came out a few minutes later to admire the progress of our decorating.

"Very nice, very nice," he murmured as I placed a lamp at the edge of a step.

My throat felt suddenly dry, but I couldn't waste this opportunity. "Thatha," I said nervously, "may I ask a question, please?"

"Of course," he said absently, looking at the red-gold line of lights.

"May I please have your permission to study in the library every evening?"

He seemed surprised at the question. "I thought we'd settled that weeks ago," he said mildly. "Of course you can." He went back indoors.

"Thank you," I called after his retreating form.

Relief poured over me like a soothing balm. I sat on the front steps, looking out at the garden, wishing I could dance like a flickering flame.

"Would you like another lamp?" amma asked. In a low voice, she added, "I'm glad you'll still be able to go to the library."

"I am too," I said, smiling at her as I placed the little light she gave me in a corner on the floor.

"Don't you think that lamp is too close to the walls?" It was Raman's voice.

I whipped around at once and grinned at him. He bent close and moved the lamp a little. "If you stick it too close to the wall, the ash from the flame will leave a mark," he said.

"Thanks," I said, happy to see him. I looked around. Only Raman, amma, Chinni chithi and I were outside. "Where's Kitta?" I asked. I hadn't spoken to my brother for weeks. "I was hoping to catch a glimpse of him today." Didn't Kitta want to see me too?

"He's probably listening to the radio," Raman said.

"I thought you only did that after dinner," I said, puzzled.

"Kitta wanted to listen to it earlier today," Raman said reluctantly.

"Why?"

"He just wanted to listen to some other stations, I think. You know."

"I don't know," I said. "What does he want to listen to the radio all the time for?"

"He's interested in hearing different points of view about the war," Raman replied.

I stared fixedly at the lamp I was holding as though deciding where to put it, trying hard to hide my disappointment at my brother's absence. Out of the corner of my eye, I saw amma and Chinni chithi rise to return indoors.

Before Chinni chithi stepped in, I asked, "Do you need help packing or anything?"

"No, but it's very sweet of you to ask," she said, turning back for a moment.

"I'll be waiting for you to come back," I said.

Chinni chithi looked pleased. "We'll miss you," she said, before leaving Raman and me on the verandah together.

Kitta wasn't there, but at least Raman was, looking at me as though he had been waiting all day for this brief moment of togetherness. I smiled up at him. Even in the twilight, I could see that the rain tree in the garden had bloomed, its feathery pink flowers splashing the world with much-needed color.

Malati's Wedding

"Get up, girl, get up!" periamma shouted into my ear at three in the morning on the first of December, the day of Malati's wedding. "Go and have your bath and come to the kitchen. Don't dawdle."

I sat up drowsily. I hadn't been in the library all week. Every evening, after school, periamma had kept me busy in the kitchen preparing special food for the wedding: pressing *appalams* until they were thin, flat circles; twisting *murukkus* into golden spirals; deep frying sweet dough to make fluffy, layered *adhirsams*. Three Brahmin cooks had been employed to help with the cooking during the weeklong wedding celebrations, but that did little to lessen the load of work periamma thrust on me.

That morning, I couldn't avoid the communal bath, but I was too tired to care. When amma came over to help me put on my sari, periamma shouted, "Leave her alone! She's not the bride! Help me dress Malati!"

Amma left at once to follow orders. I was glad Chinni chithi was gone—what a merciful custom it was to send the woman to her mother's home when she was pregnant, at least.

As soon as I entered the kitchen, periamma said, "You! Go and invite the groom's family over."

I began to move away sleepily.

"Idiot! How can you go empty-handed to invite them? Take all the necessary items. Sarasa and her husband will go with you."

"What do I need to take?" I asked.

Periamma rolled her eyes and pointed to a corner of the room. Sarasa chithi joined me.

"You can carry the coffee," she said, handing me a large *kuja* sloshing with the liquid. It was heavy, but I was thankful she knew what we had to do. She loaded up a silver tray with betel nuts, betel nut leaves, sandalwood paste and a silver container of vermilion powder.

With surprise, I saw that her husband was behind us in the kitchen. "Here," he said, taking the heavy kuja of coffee out of my hands, "I'll carry that. It's heavy and boiling hot. The *idli* vessel is a lot lighter. You carry that."

He pointed to a warm jar, probably filled with rice cakes for the groom's family's breakfast. It was still dark when we stepped out onto the verandah, where the musicians were already tuning their instruments. The *nadhaswaram* player joined our party, playing a deafening tune on his pipe. The *thavil* player followed him, banging on his drum. By the time I followed my aunt and uncle to the home three streets away, which periamma and periappa had rented for the groom's family to stay in, I was starting to have a headache.

We entered the house and I stood on the verandah, unsure of what to do. "Go and put the idlis in the kitchen and then find me," Sarasa chithi said, and we walked in together. "I will be welcoming the women to the wedding."

I set the vessel down in the kitchen gratefully, but it was only the first of what seemed like a million trips we made that morning. The groom's extended family had come for the wedding: eight brothers, two sisters, at least sixty-four cousins, a dozen aunts and uncles, grandparents and even a few grand-aunts, grand-uncles and second cousins. They all had to be fed, and so the three of us went back to fetch more coffee and more breakfast food and deliver it to the groom's family until everyone was well fed. On each trip, we were serenaded by the drummer and the piper.

I caught one fleeting glimpse of amma's harried face, and she called out, "Vidya, make sure you eat something, kanna." But before I could eat, periamma had given me another job. "Go and set up the welcoming table, and sit there until all the guests arrive," she commanded.

Two foldable tables had already been set up outside and behind them a row of foldable chairs. Raman and Kitta were sitting behind one of the tables. I had to stop myself from running up to hug Kitta. I hadn't spoken to him since Deepavali—nearly a whole month ago.

"Vidya!" Kitta shouted joyfully as soon as he saw me.

"You!" I said in mock anger. "I'm glad you still remember me."

I sat at the table opposite theirs and checked that I had everything I needed to welcome the guests with: a silver tray sparkling with sugar crystals, a flagon of rose water, a bowl filled with sandalwood paste, a small silver container with vermilion powder. I collapsed into a chair, exhausted.

Raman flashed a smile at me, and I felt a pleasant tingle in my stomach. His teeth were pearl white and beautiful.

Kitta said something, but I couldn't hear him above the din that the musicians had begun to make. They were on the verandah, but they sounded loud even where we were sitting— near the front gate.

"What?" I shouted.

"You look tired already," he yelled above the music. "Something wrong?"

"Not really," I shouted back. "Periamma got me up at three and made me run around serving the groom's family all morning, that's all."

A few minutes later, amma stopped by my table, guiding appa forward.

"You look lovely," she said.

I smiled. "So do you."

Appa turned his head in my direction, and my heart beat faster. Perhaps the din the musicians were creating had made him remember his own wedding? But he turned away again, expressionless, and they reentered the house together.

The guests began to trickle in. I splashed rose water on them as they walked past and offered them sugar. The women stopped by my table to put a pinch of vermilion powder on their foreheads and rub a bit of sandalwood paste on their necks. The men stopped at Kitta and Raman's table.

"Come in, come in," I repeated, smiling at the women until my jaws ached.

About an hour later, periappa came to the verandah and called us in, and I left my post gratefully. In the wedding bustle, there was even less adult supervision than at a festival, and Raman, Kitta and I sat together in a corner, watching as periappa repeated prayer after prayer and the Brahmin priests poured ghee into the fire altar that they had set up in the middle of the large hall of the house.

There were people everywhere—in the small hall, in the large hall, in the dining room, in the kitchen, in the women's sleeping room, on the verandah. Guests chattered incessantly except at key moments when the priests shouted out that they needed to pay attention.

"Isn't it incredible how many people can actually fit into this house?" I asked.

Raman grinned. "I heard they hired fifteen people to help this week," he said. "Your periappa told me."

I stifled a yawn as Malati left her place by the groom and went to change into her second sari of the morning, the one in which she would be married. She reappeared, decked in red and gold, and I gasped. "She's ravishing," I blurted out. As soon as I let that slip out of me, I couldn't believe I'd said that. What if Raman agreed that she looked gorgeous?

Instead, Raman looked down at me and began, "You also look—"

I stared at him in astonishment. He paused and finished with difficulty, "You also look ravishing."

I smiled at him, pretending I couldn't see Kitta, who was mouthing Raman's words at me and fluttering his eyelashes as though he were a flirtatious little girl. Raman caught him at it and cuffed him playfully.

To hide my embarrassment, I listened attentively as the bride and groom repeated the seven marriage vows in Sanskrit and took their first seven steps together as man and wife. I noticed they said the same words. The final and most important vow, the seventh, was a promise that they would go through life as best friends, always keeping in mind the other's needs and wishes.

"Our wedding vows are so equal," I exclaimed in surprise.

"Are they really?" asked Raman, looking doubtful.

"Yes," I said. "Didn't you hear them?"

"I'm very bad at Sanskrit," he confessed, looking sheepish. "So the wife doesn't promise to obey the husband? I thought that's what she had to do."

"You think a woman should obey her man?" I asked.

"No, not necessarily," he said.

"Not necessarily?" I asked, pressing him for more.

He paused. "No, I don't think she needs to," he said. "Why should she? I just never really thought about it before."

I pressed him further. "What do you mean? What do you mean you never thought of it before?"

Raman was quiet for a while. "I don't have any sisters, and I never spent a lot of time thinking about the way we do things," he said. "Not until I met you."

Kitta fluttered his eyelashes at me again. This time, Raman pinned my brother's arms to his sides, and I punched Kitta lightly on his nose. Kitta made a funny face, and the three of us laughed.

We walked out to the verandah together and sat down by the welcoming benches again. I noticed a basket filled with coconuts had been set down beside each bench. After the guests had eaten their lunch and before they left, we would have to give them parting gifts of coconuts and betel nut leaves. But there were hours until then.

I looked across at Raman. Sunshine drizzled onto his shoulders through the dappled shade cast by the overhanging branches of the rain tree. We were, all three of us, enveloped in gold. I felt as bright as a ray of sunlight.

Malati's Departure

The week flew by. Periamma had me stay home from school and attend to the groom's family until the *shanthi kalyanam,* the final day of prayer before the bride and groom consummated their marriage. The next morning, after I awoke, I couldn't stop smiling. It was a day I had been waiting for. The groom had spent the last night at the bride's home, as he was supposed to according to tradition. In a few hours, he and Malati would be gone from the house!

Malati was dressed in a parrot green silk sari with jasmine flowers in her braid. "She looks beautiful," I said to Kitta.

Kitta disagreed. "Actually, she looks really sad to me."

"Sad?" I asked, staring closely at Malati as she and her husband prostrated themselves before thatha to ask his blessing. When she stood up, I saw that Kitta was right. Malati's normally dazzling eyes were the color of the sky before sunset. She had been crying.

My chest felt tight. I wanted to shrink and hide myself away. I had been celebrating her departure, waiting for it, glad

I would hardly ever see her again. I never thought that she might have been scared by all the changes she would have to make when she moved away. However much she wanted to get married, there must have been times when it had felt overwhelming and frightening.

The family began walking toward the verandah to see the couple off. Periamma and periappa had arranged for a car, in which they would accompany their daughter to the groom's home. They would leave her behind and come back alone.

Periappa walked down the steps carrying Malati's suitcases. The groom followed him. Periamma was already in the car. I saw Malati hang back and look at the house intently, as though she were photographing it in her mind—the way it looked the day she left it for good.

"Malati," I said softly, stepping in beside her, "there's something I want to tell you."

I could see that she was fighting her tears.

"I know we weren't friends, but I wish you well," I said. "He seems a good man, your husband, and I hope you'll be very happy with him."

She gave me an astonished look.

"I mean it," I said. "I wish you only the best."

For a moment she gazed at me as though trying to determine if I was joking or telling the truth. Then she smiled uncertainly.

"Thank you," she said, and started to walk down the front steps. Before she stepped into the car, she turned back, walked up the steps and said to me quietly, "I'm sorry I didn't welcome you to this house. But I wish you well too."

The car raised a cloud of dust as Malati and her parents and her husband drove off. The rest of the family went indoors, except for Kitta, Raman and me. The three of us lingered behind on the verandah, enjoying a companionable silence. We were exhausted—the wedding had kept us all busy.

After a while, Kitta announced that he was going indoors.

"Want to go up to the library?" Raman asked.

I shook my head. "I think I just want to stay out here and enjoy the sunshine a little longer," I said.

"All right," he said. "I'm going indoors, though. It's getting a little too hot for me out here."

They left me sitting by myself. A little procession of red ants was wandering near my feet, carrying away lumps of sugar. A child had probably been eating wedding sweets on the verandah and dropped some. I thought of the size of the burdens the ants carried on their backs, so much larger than their tiny bodies.

The sound of a car horn brought me back to the moment. Periamma and periappa were back, alone.

I stood up slowly, expecting periamma to shout at me for sitting out on the verandah on my own.

She didn't. Making no sign that she had even registered my

presence, she walked up and collapsed into a huddle on the lowest step. She began to shake uncontrollably, sobs bursting out of her.

I took a step toward her hesitantly.

"My Malati is gone," she wailed. "My daughter is gone."

I walked toward her and laid my hand on her head, but I didn't know what to say. Her back shuddered. Her tears were wetting her sari. I tried gingerly to wipe them off with the *pallu,* the free end of my half sari.

"Periamma," I whispered. "Please don't cry."

It was as if a stone fruit had cracked, exposing the soft, vulnerable flesh beneath its armor-hard exterior.

"Please, tell me how I can help." I stroked her hair, feeling awkward.

She stiffened.

Then periappa walked up to us. Without acknowledging my presence, he sat down with periamma. "You mustn't cry," he said to her gruffly, though his own eyes were brimming. "It's a good match. She'll be very happy."

Periamma nodded, but she wailed again, louder than ever. Periappa repeated what he had said before, again and again, as tears began to streak his own cheeks.

I was an intruder in their private grief. I stepped back. Before I entered the house, I prayed silently that Malati should have a happy married life.

Pearl Harbor

Immediately after Malati's departure, periamma seemed more subdued than in the past. She did not order us around as much that evening. At first, I thought she liked me more now because I'd reached out to her. I tried to help around the house, to be sensitive to her needs, to not get in her way. But just two days later, things were back to normal. In fact, she even seemed worse than ever, as though she hated me twice as much for having seen her moment of weakness.

I managed to escape to the library the first day of her relapse to bad behavior, protected by thatha's permission. My eyes fell on Sri Aurobindo's *The Secret of the Veda,* a book I thought I remembered appa mentioning to Kitta long ago.

The book was as beautifully written as it was profound. I was so deeply immersed in the first chapter that I hardly noticed when Kitta burst in.

"Have you heard the news, Vidya?" Kitta asked. "The Japanese bombed Pearl Harbor a few days back. I didn't find out until now because everyone was so busy with the wedding. America has joined the war."

"Pearl Harbor?" I was confused. "What's that?"

"It's an American naval base," Kitta explained. "The Americans consider Japan's bombing an act of war."

Kitta watched to see what effect his proclamation had. I didn't really know what to think or say. "Is that good?" I asked.

"I think it is," Kitta said. "I think America might just give the Allies the edge they need to actually win."

A half hour later, Raman found me listening to Kitta, who was expounding on allied tactics and possible future combat scenarios. Kitta had evidently become more obsessed than ever with the war.

Raman smiled at me and waited patiently for Kitta to run out of things to say. Then he turned to me with a shy smile. "I might go to America next year," he said.

He caught me by surprise. "You might go to America?" I repeated dumbly.

"That's right," he said. "To get my master's degree. I applied to a school in Boston called the Massachusetts Institute of Technology."

I looked down at the floor for a while and said nothing.

"It's a really good college," Kitta put in. "It's every bit as good as Cambridge and Oxford."

"Why?" I asked finally.

"Why America instead of England, you mean?" Raman asked. "I don't feel like going to England. At least America used to be a colony once. Like we are now."

"Oh," I said.

"The Americans kicked the British out, just a bunch of untrained farmers firing at them with muskets," Kitta said.

"We'll kick the Brits out too," I said. "Though our farmers won't use muskets."

Kitta shrugged, looked into my face and then decided to leave me and Raman alone together.

I was at a loss for words. I knew I ought to wish Raman good luck or encourage him in his dreams for the future. I said in what I hoped was a cheerful tone, "So tell me something about America and their colleges and everything."

Raman talked about the college he'd applied to and how good it was and how impressed he'd been when he read the American Declaration of Independence from Britain. He talked about Thoreau, an American whom he said Gandhiji respected.

But at that moment, I didn't care about Thoreau. "When will you leave?" I asked unhappily.

"If I go, I'll probably have to sail out in August next year," he continued. "Their academic year starts much later than ours. In September, I think."

"How long will you be away?" I asked.

"At least two years," he said.

I couldn't imagine two years without him. I fixed my eyes on the geometric pattern of my half sari and twisted the cloth between my fingers.

"How can you go?" I asked. "Aren't the seas unsafe because of the war?"

Raman shrugged. "Unsafe? Yes. But then, we have to keep on doing things, don't we? We can't just stop living because of the war."

"No, I suppose not," I said. I could feel his eyes on me. I avoided his gaze.

"Didn't the white Americans exterminate the natives?" I asked, trying desperately to find a reason why it wasn't a suitable place for Raman to move to. "The ones they call Red Indians?"

Raman shrugged. "No country is perfect," he said.

I stared at my feet, trying to find some other objection. "The whites there enslaved Africans, didn't they?"

"The Americans outlawed slavery years ago," Raman said.

A starless dusk was gathering. I peered out into the cold, clammy gloom. Raman started talking excitedly again, about America and how young it was.

For once, I didn't really listen to him. I felt as if I were locked in a dark, walled cell. I didn't want Raman to leave, and yet there was nothing I could do to stop him.

Pongal

Raman soon realized that his possible departure for America was not my favorite topic of conversation, and he veered away from it. Our conversations entered safer waters again, meandering frequently into discussions on Indian philosophers. Raman surprised me by telling me that Sri Aurobindo, whose book on the Vedas was so large that I was taking weeks to finish it, had once been part of a violent protest against the British government and that he had found his spirituality when he was thrown into solitary confinement. Sometimes we discussed the progress of our freedom struggle and the men and women who battled valiantly on, even after the British locked our most charismatic leaders behind bars.

I saw little of Kitta during the month between Malati's departure and the festival of Pongal in mid-January. He joined me and Raman in the library only rarely. When he did, he spoke mostly about the latest developments on the various war fronts.

On the morning of Pongal, the harvest festival, the entire

family gathered together in the kitchen. Periamma set a pot of new rice on the stove, and we watched it bubble over as it cooked.

"*Pongalo, pongal!*" Raman shouted enthusiastically, and all our voices followed his in the joyful cry of thanks for the year's harvest. I even thought I saw a faint smile on appa's face. Could he possibly be getting better?

I looked more closely, and his face was expressionless again. I realized I'd probably just imagined it, but somehow I still felt strangely happy. Before breakfast, periamma made me stir a big pot of rice with roasted cashew nuts and raisins and clumps of unrefined brown sugar until the rice dripped with sweetness and my arms ached, but even that didn't spoil my mood.

On the second day of Pongal, I awoke at five because I didn't want to miss seeing the milkman's cow, which would be decorated specially for the festival. I rushed out of the house as soon as I heard the tinkle of bells. The maid was up already, splashing the front steps with water, preparing to draw a fresh festive kolam. I smiled at her and ran past her toward the gate, where the milkman was waiting. His cow tossed its head, its freshly painted yellow horns gleaming like gold in the soft light of the dawn.

Within minutes of my arrival, the other women gathered outside. I watched periamma put vermilion powder on the cow's forehead. Someone poked my shoulder and I turned around. It was Kitta.

I smiled at him and walked away from the rest of the family. Raman wasn't there yet, and it was a long time since I'd spoken to Kitta alone.

"Kitta," I said. "Can you stay outside for a bit? I want to talk to you."

He nodded.

"What's Raman like, really?" I asked. The cow stamped its hooves, and the anklets on its legs jangled loudly. I kept my voice low to make sure no one could overhear me.

"What do you mean?" Kitta asked.

"You spend so much more time with Raman than I do," I said. "You know him better than I do."

"Maybe, maybe not," Kitta said noncommittally.

"It's just that he's so—" I tried to think of what it was that worried me about him. "Sometimes he says things that are—"

"Vidya," amma called. It was my turn to pet the cow. I walked over and stroked its soft fur. Its nose was wet. I took a pinch of vermilion powder from the container amma was holding and applied it to the cow's head. The milkman smiled at me.

The women went indoors. I returned to where Kitta was standing, still a little way off, by himself. But before I could talk to him, he asked, "What do you think about war?"

I stared at him. "Why?" I asked.

Kitta didn't exactly answer. "I've been discussing things with one of my professors at college," he said. "Can you fight without hate in the heart if it's your dharma, your duty?"

"Do you have to write an essay about that?" I said distractedly. I wanted to talk about Raman.

"No," he said. "I just want to know what you think."

"Where did that question come from?" I asked.

"Just answer me, Vidya, please."

I shrugged. "You can't fight without hate," I said. "That's rubbish. Killing is wrong. That's all there is to it."

Raman emerged from the house and joined us, but Kitta didn't even greet him. "What if by killing one evil man like Hitler, you stop the murder of innocent thousands?" he asked me.

"Give me an example of a war in which just one evil person was killed," I said, giving him my most withering look.

"Lots of people are dying in this war, but I think it's an important one to fight," Kitta said unhesitatingly.

"So if you already know that this war is good, why bother asking me about it?" I demanded.

"I don't know," Kitta said slowly. "I just wonder about everything. What Gandhiji says. What appa believed. It just doesn't seem like nonviolence works sometimes."

"You know better than Gandhiji?" I asked, looking at Raman for support.

"I'm not saying that," Kitta continued. "I'm just saying in this case, violence seems to be the only answer." Raman turned his head away.

"Hitler the great oppressor, fought off by the English, who never oppressed anyone, of course, as we all know," I said in a voice drenched with sarcasm.

"The British play by rules," Kitta said. "Not necessarily fair rules, not always good ones, but rules of some kind."

I was shocked. How could Kitta defend the men who had all but killed our father? Appa had been his father as much as mine.

"The British are far better than the Germans," Kitta insisted stubbornly.

"Are they?" I shouted. "Have you forgotten what they did to appa? You think appa's way is weak just because it killed him? I don't. I think it's the bravest way to be, appa's way."

Kitta didn't meet my gaze. He insisted, "In spite of everything, the British are not as bad."

I couldn't believe he had said that. "You don't care about appa!" I yelled recklessly.

Kitta glared. "I care for appa every day!" he yelled back. "I'm the one who looks after him, remember? You act like appa's dead. Who are you to talk about respecting him?" He stormed past me into the house.

Rage welled up inside me like steam trapped in a closed vessel. I found the edge of my pallu and pulled at the thin fabric with all my strength. It ripped apart angrily. I tore it again and again and again until it was shredded into tiny pieces.

"Vidya, what are you so angry about?" Raman's tone was gentle. I looked up. He was standing only a few feet away.

I wanted to say I was angry about everything—the house, the school, Madras. I hated that I couldn't talk to my mother anymore and that my brother was acting strange.

Raman sat down, leaving a safe distance between us. I fidgeted, staring at the torn end of the sari, feeling ashamed of myself for what I had done to make appa lose his mind, for shredding my pallu in front of Raman. I wanted to say I hated myself most of all, but my throat was choking and I couldn't speak.

"Vidya, talk to me," Raman said softly. He made a move as though he wanted to come closer to me but stopped. "You're thinking of your father," he said. "Aren't you?"

I nodded. "He'd still be here if it hadn't been for me," I heard myself say.

"You speak about him as if he's dead," Raman said. "But he isn't. He's still here."

"I'm responsible," I said. "It's my fault he was beaten." I wanted to talk to him, tell him everything, but I was scared. Scared, the way I was scared about what amma or Kitta would say if they knew my part in what had happened at the protest march.

"No," he said, his voice fierce but barely above a whisper.

"I was there," I said. "I made it happen. I hate myself."

"Vidya," he said. "Don't be silly now."

I saw the protest march again, appa holding the strange lady, protecting her. I saw the policeman's lathi. I heard its thwacking sound. I shuddered.

"Vidya," Raman said. "Let it go."

I couldn't. But somehow, in spite of the weight inside me, in spite of the distance between me and Raman, though he could not hold my hand, I felt a sense of comfort.

"Vidya." I felt amma's touch on my shoulder. "Come in. We're going to the terrace to feed the crows."

I got up and followed her all the way to the terrace on the topmost floor with the other women. Earlier that morning, I'd been thrilled that we'd be allowed up there because of the festival. But all my excitement had since drained out of me. As I rolled out small balls of rice—brown, turmeric yellow, vermilion red and white—and set them in odd-numbered rows on a glistening, green, clean turmeric leaf, I thought about the fight I'd had with Kitta.

I saw amma close her eyes and murmur the traditional prayer to the crows, the prayer for unity in the family.

I closed my own eyes and prayed fervently that I should regain the closeness I'd shared with Kitta. And though Raman was not a relative, I prayed that he and I should never grow apart.

Air-Raid Drills

The next day, the small room downstairs where the men listened to the news at night was converted into an air-raid shelter. Construction workers came during the day and reinforced the room's ceiling with wooden beams. Periamma made me hang bits of black cloth on all the lights, complaining that the British had also begun to ration our food. Amma covered all the windows with brown paper.

A week after Pongal, just after the men had been served dinner, I heard a strange, incessant whine.

"What's happening?" periamma cried in fear.

"It's just an air-raid precaution drill," thatha said. He got up slowly. "Everyone into the small hall," he said. "I'll turn the lights off as soon as we're in."

I stood inside the kitchen, watching.

"Go," thatha ordered. "Children first. Vidya, leave the rice where it is and go in. Take your mother with you."

I linked my arm through amma's, but she was unwilling to move. "Kitta," she said. Kitta was pulling appa's arm. He stood up and followed Kitta obediently. We entered the room together. I sat down on one of the sandbags that lined the wall. Kitta settled in close beside me, our recent argument forgotten. Raman joined us.

I saw appa's face just before thatha turned the light off in the room. Appa didn't look scared, though the siren was wailing now as though it would never go off.

"We have to practice in case the Japanese bomb us?" I whispered into Kitta's ear.

"Yes," he said. I thought he sounded angry. "Yes, that's what we're practicing for."

"But aren't they still far away, Kitta?" I whispered. The siren's wail was unnerving. I wanted to run somewhere, not just sit indoors and hear it moaning.

Kitta's laugh was harsh. "The Japs are getting closer and closer," he said. "And here we are, waiting for them to walk into India and take it."

"They won't reach India," Raman said. His voice was weak.

"Why would they want India?" I asked. The room was stifling with all the windows shut.

Kitta's harsh laugh sounded again. "The same reason we've been conquered and raped by the British," he said.

His tone shocked me into silence. I felt beads of sweat bursting on my forehead.

"India is rich with resources," he said. "We have manpower.

More than a hundred thousand Indian volunteers are serving in this war. We have coal. We have iron. We make steel for armor plate and guns and shells and ammunition. Britain needs us."

"How do you know all that?" I asked, mopping the back of my sweat-drenched neck with the pallu of my half sari.

Kitta ignored me. "If the Japanese conquer India, they might as well have won the war. Without India, the Allies will lose."

"But the Japanese are still in Burma, aren't they?" I said. The headlines of *The Hindu* had screamed about that takeover. "Burma isn't nearby."

"Burma is not that far from Calcutta," Kitta said. "The Japanese will fight for the Bay of Bengal as soon as they settle down in Burma. They'll take Siam and enter the Andaman Islands. And once they have India, they'll have access to Russia and China and the Middle East. Hitler's already invaded Russia from one end—he can split his spoils with the Japs."

Hearing his voice in the darkness, the war sounded frighteningly close all of a sudden, the war I had ignored for so long.

"How do you know all that?" I asked again. "How can you be so sure?"

"I talk to people in college," he said. "My professors. My

classmates. India is a prize, an industrial and strategic prize. We're the jewel in the British crown. The Japanese know that."

I wanted to hear Raman say something to contradict Kitta, to tell Kitta he was talking nonsense, that his facts were all wrong. But Raman was silent.

"All over Southeast Asia, the British are losing to the Japanese," Kitta continued. "They'll take Singapore and Ceylon, and then they'll march into Madras. Meanwhile we'll be sitting here, doing nothing."

"Don't be silly, Kitta," I said. "You've become such a pessimist."

"I haven't," he said. "I just pay attention to what's happening outside this house. I think about what my teachers tell me."

We sat together in a tense silence. My head was hurting when the siren went off again—a steady sound this time, not the horrid wail.

"That's the all clear," thatha said, turning on the light. "We can return to our supper now."

We filed back into the dining room, and I picked up the rice container. My hand trembled uncontrollably as I served Raman.

Raman looked up with concern, and for the first time, he spoke directly to me in the dining room even though everyone else was listening. "Don't worry," he said, "the Axis won't take us over."

His voice lacked conviction.

I peered intently into his eyes. Normally they soothed me; it was like looking at the waters of a calm lake. This time, I could see a storm of fear building beneath the limpid surface.

The Dark Fortnight

The first week of February was filled with air-raid drills, and though I hardly enjoyed them, they gave me much greater contact with Kitta than I'd had over the past months. I tried to steer his mind away from gloomy prognostications about the Japanese. Raman often joined in and tried to support my efforts to introduce lighter topics of conversation, but we were largely unsuccessful.

The nights grew darker as the moon waned, and on a moonless night in mid-February the household gathered again to observe Sivarathri, the night of prayer and meditation.

I was tired that evening after school, and I wondered how I would manage to spend the entire night in prayer as we were supposed to do. Periamma announced that all the men of the house were going to attend a retelling of a religious story, a *kathakalakshepam*. It was one way to stay up, though it was entertainment, not prayer. I saw Kitta and Raman leaving the house, holding appa by his hand. I wished I could get out of the house too, but that method of keeping awake all night wasn't an option given to women.

I found Sarasa chithi and periamma in the women's sleeping hall. They were sitting cross-legged on the floor, face-to-face, playing *pallanguzhi* with cowrie shells as though they were little children. I walked toward them because I didn't feel like praying.

"Don't you have anything better to do?" periamma asked me as I sat down between them. But she didn't tell me to leave.

She started placing the cowrie shells on the ground. Sarasa chithi won the first game and the second.

As periamma set the shells down for the third round, Sarasa chithi said to her, as though I wasn't there, "You know, I've been meaning to tell you, there's an excellent match I thought about for Vidya. My brother's wife's cousin is a slow boy; you know what I mean? He must be about ten years older than Vidya."

Periamma looked up at her. "Dim-witted, is he?"

Sarasa chithi nodded.

"So they would be willing, you think, to take a girl with an idiot father?"

I wanted to say something, but my tongue felt too stiff to move.

"Yes, yes," Sarasa chithi went on. "They aren't very rich, so they'll be glad to have her dowry, and they need an extra pair of hands in that house, I believe."

I managed to get up.

"Where are you going, girl?" periamma demanded.

"She must be tired of losing," Sarasa chithi said in a high-pitched voice. She giggled.

"Don't think you can go to sleep," periamma said. "You are supposed to stay awake all night."

"Stay awake praying all night, not playing games," I muttered under my breath.

"What was that?" periamma asked sharply.

I walked away. I needed to talk to amma while periamma and Sarasa chithi played games together. This was one night when we might actually be able to converse privately.

I found amma in the poojai room, praying with her eyes closed. I sat down beside her. She was praying so intently she hardly noticed me. I waited for amma to open her eyes, but she didn't.

"Amma," I said at last. "Amma, can I talk to you?"

She opened her eyes, and I saw the nest of lines that had deepened around them. "It's nothing," I mumbled. "Never mind."

She looked searchingly into my face. "What is it, kanna?"

"Amma, I'm scared thatha is going to arrange my marriage now that Malati's gone," I blurted out.

"Scared?" she asked gently. "Why, Vidya?"

"I don't want to get married," I said. I struggled to tell her how much I wanted to study, to go to college.

But before I could, she put her arm around my shoulders

and said, "Marriage is nothing to be afraid, of, Vidya. It was the best thing that happened to me, becoming your father's wife."

"But appa was different," I said. "Most Brahmin men aren't like him."

"Yes, he is wonderful, your father," she said, not listening to me fully. "I will pray for you all the rest of this night, Vidya, that you will soon be married to a man like him."

"Amma, I don't want to marry anyone," I said. "They'll marry me to someone horrible, I know they will."

"Of course not," she said, patting my cheek.

Before I could say more, she closed her eyes. I watched her lips move, murmuring a prayer. She did not open them to speak to me again.

A part of me wanted to shake her and make her listen to me. Another part of me was upset at how frail she looked. I tried to follow her example and think of God, but I couldn't pray. Instead, I tried to talk to God. I tried to meditate on Shakthi, powerful consort of Siva, whose splendor we celebrated that night. Shakthi, the source of mental and spiritual strength. I imagined her sitting beside me.

I told her about Raman and how confused he made me feel: sometimes he was my best friend, and other times he scared me because there was so much he didn't question. I asked her to show me a way to bridge the rift that was widening between me and Kitta. I asked for forgiveness for my thoughtless actions during the protest march.

At some point during that conversation, I started to pray in earnest. I prayed that a soul still lingered within the shell of body now left to my father, that I would find a way to speak to him again. I prayed that I would find the strength to grow even in this house, like a plant I had seen growing through a crack in the terrace wall. I prayed until the first thin lavender tresses of dawn began to creep into the sky.

I opened my eyes again when I heard the men returning and walked out of the poojai room to the front hall. Kitta came up to me. "Vidya," he said. "I want to tell you something."

Before he could say any more, periamma shouted, "Girl! Get ready to serve breakfast!"

Kitta gave me an unhappy look, squared his shoulders and walked toward our grandfather. In a voice that was louder than usual, he said, "I need your blessing."

"You already have it," thatha said absently.

"I mean, I need your blessing for what I'm going to do next. I'm going to join the Indian troops."

The silence in the room was broken by amma's strangled gasp.

"Enlist in the British army?" periappa asked.

"The British Indian Army. Against the Axis," Kitta said.

"Are you mad?" Chinni chithi's husband asked softly. "The British almost murdered your father."

"But you say all the time that the Nazis are worse than the British, don't you?" Kitta said, seemingly unperturbed.

Every man in the room began to shout, their voices rising to a crescendo.

"Foolish boy!"

"Ungrateful wretch!"

"British spy!"

"Brahmins have no place in the army. We are meant to be scholars, not soldiers," thatha said.

"Caste is a social evil, not a religious law." Kitta's voice, calm and steady, rose above the excited babble, like a mountain unperturbed by the gale that was blowing about its sides.

"Stain your hands with blood, boy, and I will never receive you in my house," periappa shouted. Breaking away from the rabble, he ran toward Kitta. The muscles in Kitta's upper arm flexed. He pushed periappa away.

Never before had I ever seen Kitta behave disrespectfully with any family member. My heart stood still as I saw the strange tableau—Kitta and periappa standing in the middle of the hall, their hands raised above their shoulders, locked together in anger, pushing at each other.

Thatha said nothing. Neither did Raman.

I looked at Kitta's long, delicate fingers, interlocked with periappa's. I could not imagine them curled around a rifle.

"Kitta," amma gasped. "Don't leave us." Her face was gray as the sacred ash she wore in a horizontal streak across her forehead.

Kitta took a step toward her. She swayed on her feet. I ran forward and steadied her with both arms.

Kitta moved closer to us. Thatha stepped in front of him, his back to us, tall and straight as a temple tower.

I could see Kitta staring into thatha's eyes. His gaze was pleading. "Thatha," he said softly. "Please understand."

The room fell silent. Amma closed her eyes. My arms ached from holding her. She put her hand against the wall and then sank down slowly to her feet and sat with her back propped up against it. I heard a crow cawing somewhere in the garden.

"If you join their army," thatha said tonelessly, "you will be dead to me and the rest of this family. Forever."

Kitta's eyes hardened. He crossed his arms in front of him. The muscles of his cheek tensed. "I must leave," he said.

Thatha glared at him, but Kitta stared back steadily, unblinkingly.

"Then get out and don't ever come back." Thatha's voice was quiet. An order that would never be overturned.

Kitta's Choice

I made my way out of the room as though I were sleepwalking. My feet carried me to the library, and I stood and looked out of the window.

Someone turned me around gently. I stared into Kitta's face. "Well, what does my sister think?" he asked.

"I never thought my brother would become a murderer," I said.

"I've told you a thousand times. Hitler is a crazy fanatic. The Japanese will be on Indian soil any minute now. Should we all just wait and watch?"

"What about this?" I pulled the slim translation of the *Dhammapada* off the shelf and flung it at him. "What about what the Buddha said about peace?"

"Don't throw books about," he said, raising it to his eyes respectfully and replacing it carefully on the shelf. "Books are sacred."

"Don't kill," I retorted. "Life is sacred."

"When do you think we should act?" he asked. "After they've bombed Madras into smithereens?"

"The British destroyed appa and you want to fight on their side?"

"It won't be easy. It was the hardest choice I ever had to make."

"You're a traitor," I shouted.

"No," he said calmly. "When the war is over, I'll return to fight for our independence."

I wanted to scream and shake him. "You would never have done this if appa were alive."

"In case you haven't noticed recently, our father *is* still alive," he said.

I could feel tears welling up, but I would not let them fall. Images were racing through my mind, making me dizzy. Amma, appa, Kitta and I, together at Mahim beach. The four of us together in our garden in Bombay. Sitting together, speaking together. We were in pieces now. Kitta wouldn't even have thought of enlisting if appa was in his right mind. Appa would have stopped Kitta somehow.

"What will I do here without you?" I asked him.

"Is that really all you care about?" he asked. "The petty battles women fight under this roof?"

"What do you care about?" I countered. "You don't care about anything—not me, not amma, not appa, not India— nothing."

"I care about the world, Vidya. The whole world needs our help in this war."

"One man won't make a difference," I said. "Most Indians aren't fighting for the British, they're fighting against them."

"We Indians are the largest all-volunteer force in this war," he said proudly.

I thought of the courage with which appa had fought before he had been beaten. It was a noble way to fight. I saw it more clearly now than ever. Appa was braver than any soldier on any battlefield. "Appa died believing in nonviolence," I said. "If you join the army, you'll betray everything he stood for."

"Nonviolence doesn't work quickly, Vidya. We can't afford to wait any longer if we want to preserve the future of humanity."

"Thatha can lock you up in this house. He can make you stay," I tried.

"Can't you understand why I'm going away? Jews are fleeing Germany like flies, and there's nowhere for them to go. Hitler is mad. The Italians and Japanese are crazy too at the moment."

"Who cares about Jews?" My voice quavered. "Don't you care about your own people?"

"Wasn't your friend Rifka Indian? Wasn't she Jewish too?"

I swallowed. "Yes. Fine. So the Jews can come here. We've

sheltered them for centuries. Rifka said India was always a haven for Jewish refugees."

"India was. British India isn't. And this war is bigger than any one group of people. It's about challenging the worst dictator the world has ever known."

"You're exaggerating. You're just trying to convince yourself. And me."

"Why would I do that?" Kitta lowered his voice. "You can always tell when I'm lying."

I looked at him and knew he was telling the truth. Or what he thought was the truth. But I didn't care. He wasn't going to win me over.

"They'll make me marry," I said. Suddenly the only thing that mattered was that I would be alone.

"No one can make you do something you don't want to," he said, his voice softening.

"I need you here," I begged. "I need you to preserve my sanity. My future."

"You don't need me," he said.

"Please, Kitta. Stay for my sake. Please." I clutched at his arm.

He shook off my grip. "You'll be fine. You can live without me. You should learn to be independent."

"I hate you," I whispered, hot tears of anger spurting from my eyes.

"Good. Then you won't mind if I leave."

I turned my face to the wall. I listened to his footfall as he crossed the hall.

"You'd never have left if appa was still here," I shouted. My voice echoed in the empty room.

He would turn back, he had to turn back. But he didn't. His steps faded into silence.

Alone

I didn't go to school that day. I stayed in the library, not even going down at lunchtime.

I tried to look for comfort in the *Dhammapada,* but I couldn't keep my mind on Lord Buddha's words. After staring at a page sightlessly for an hour, I put it away and took out the book Raman had given me. *Rifka,* I wrote, *Kitta's left us. He's enlisted in the British Indian Army.* I couldn't write anything else. A huge blue ink blot dripped out of my pen, half obliterating the sentence I had written. The pen's point pierced through the soaked paper. I capped the pen, put it away, and then I drew my knees close to my body and rested my chin on them. I chanted every prayer I knew under my breath.

Darkness was closing in, cutting out the light like a curtain, when it finally sank into me—the realization that my brother had left.

Forever.

Venus was shining brightly in the purpling sky when Raman came up and found me hunched up on the window seat, hugging my knees. I turned to look at him without the usual flutter in my chest when I caught sight of his handsome features. All emotion had drained out of me.

"Vidya," he said. "I'm sorry. I wish there was something I could have done."

I said nothing.

"Kitta made me promise I wouldn't tell you. He didn't want you to know ahead of time. He didn't want you to get upset."

"Kitta told *you*?" The feeling of betrayal slapped me like a cold wave. "He told you and not me? He told you and you didn't stop him?"

"I couldn't stop him, Vidya. No one can. He's a grown man."

"He was your friend and you let him go," I said accusingly.

"I didn't just let him go. We discussed it. He felt deeply about the war," Raman said.

"If you think what he's doing is right, then why don't you go too?"

"I don't think it's right, Vidya. To me nonviolence is more than a philosophy. It's a way to live. I can't pull a trigger against anyone for any reason. But he feels differently, and I can't change that."

My voice was shrill. "How long has he been thinking about it?"

"For some months now, at least."

"How could you let him? How could you?" I pleaded.

"Vidya, please—" He broke off.

I sat in a shocked silence, holding my head in my hands. How was it that I had let Kitta go? I needed to see him again.

"Vidya, I tried. I—" He broke off again and sank into the chair by the writing desk. I felt numb. I hardly noticed when Raman rose and left.

My eyes were used to the dark by the time I stumbled back down the stairs again.

Amma was awake. Waiting for me in the shadows. She stepped out as I approached the sleeping hall.

"Vidya," she whispered.

I pretended not to hear, but she came to me and took my hand.

"You must eat something."

I shook my head, but she led me out of the room and I allowed her to force me to sit in the dark kitchen and eat some curds and rice. She tried to speak, but I did not respond.

I stretched out on the ground beside the quietly breathing bodies after supper, staring at the ceiling.

In the darkness, I could barely make out amma's form. Her body was trembling. I knew she was crying, but I was too upset to comfort her.

When I closed my eyes, I had a vision of Kitta's face covered in blood. He was in the dense Burmese jungle being shot at by Japanese. He was on the African grassland shooting at soldiers who wore swastika-decorated armbands. He was trying to climb a Middle Eastern desert dune. He was wearing a policeman's uniform, standing helplessly beside an officer who was shooting at appa.

I needed to try and bring him back. I had to.

Saidapet

I got up before the first ray of sunlight pierced the bruised, blue-black sky. I raised myself on one elbow. At the far end of the room, I could see Sarasa chithi's stomach wobbling like a mass of solidified curd. Periamma was not snoring in her usual place.

Surely she had not woken up so early? She never did. Then I realized that it was probably periamma's night in the couple room. I shuddered slightly, pushing away the image of periamma and periappa engaged in a sweaty night meeting. It was good that periamma was in the couple room. That meant she would be up later than usual this morning.

I got to my feet but did not roll up my mat. Instead, I picked my way carefully between the sleeping figures. The painted green double doors creaked as I pushed them apart. Sarasa chithi rolled over and I held my breath, watching until her body rose and fell again in a gentle motion.

I slipped between the doors. The hall was empty. I heard a cough emanate from the couple room and quickened my pace, moving rapidly across the cool mosaic floor. I was at the foot of the stairway, and I climbed fast.

I had never seen the library before dawn. It was dark, silent, mysterious. A circle of pale, cream-yellow light dripped into the room near the window seat, like a patch of molten ghee. I crept toward it and felt for the familiar shelf, thankful I had chosen a hiding place that was close to the only source of natural light in the room. Surely this fat leather-bound volume was the Scott?

I pulled it out with both hands carefully and then reached into the empty space behind the volume until I felt the silken material of the drawstring pouch in which I had been collecting the money I saved on the bus rides to school and back every day. My fingers closed over it tightly, but as I pulled it out, the coins jingled. I placed the book back in on the shelf and tied the pouch tight, crushing the spare cloth around it to muffle the jingling coins. Could I manage to sneak it down and into my schoolbag without anyone noticing? I grabbed a map of Madras city, folded it and stuck it in the pouch.

My heart was pounding like a drum as I returned to the sleeping room and stuffed the pouch into the bottom of my bag. No one was awake. Suddenly tired, I lay down on the mat again, closing my eyes for a few quiet moments until it was time to get up and pick flowers for periamma's morning poojai.

With every flower I picked, I murmured a silent prayer. Not the customary apology to the flower, but a fervent prayer to the universe to help me bring Kitta back. As periamma's voice rose into the morning air, I prayed silently, my eyes closed, concentrating on the image of Ganesha, remover of obstacles. I thanked him that Malati had decided to drop out of school. I thanked him that I'd had the good sense to save some of my bus fare.

Amma's hand trembled as she served the men breakfast.

"You should rest," Thatha said to her gruffly. "Don't work today."

Periamma glared, but amma returned to the kitchen and sat huddled in a corner.

"First the son leaves, then the mother decides to take a holiday from work," periamma muttered, but she could not overrule thatha. "You, girl. Make yourself useful!" she yelled at me instead.

When the women sat down to eat, amma stared listlessly at her food and said nothing. Periamma said loudly, "No loyalty, that boy had. Didn't anyone tell him that Brahmins aren't meant to touch weapons?"

"It's his upbringing," Sarasa chithi said at once. "He was obviously never taught to tell right from wrong."

"We are supposed to set an example to the rest of society," periamma said. "Army people have a debauched lifestyle. Maybe that's why the boy left. So he could enjoy all those things we don't allow in a respectable Brahmin household."

Sarasa chithi tittered.

I was too preoccupied to argue. My stomach felt strangely taut, but I knew I had to eat. I forced some idli down my throat, wishing I could pack a few of the spongy rice cakes away unnoticed for the journey.

I walked to the bus stop and climbed nervously into the bus. The khaki-clad conductor tore off my usual ticket and handed it to me before I could say anything. My hand shook slightly as I took it.

I got off as usual, one stop before school. But instead of walking to class, I sat down on a low bench and opened the map. It took me a while to find where I was. I wasn't very good at reading it. But after poring over it for some time, I decided to go to Saidapet because it was near a police station. The bus line that dropped me off at school ended somewhere called the Saidapet Bus Terminus.

I got into the next bus and asked for a ticket to the terminus. The bus bumped along rickety roads before grinding to its final stop. The bus emptied. I was the last one to leave the security of its walls. I stood and looked at the bustling confusion around me, wondering where I should go.

There were people everywhere and stray dogs and chickens. I saw beggars, hordes of them: children with faces disfigured by smallpox, women who were bent over like bows, old men skinny as arrows, young people lacking limbs.

"*Akka, kaasu kudunga, akka.* Sister, give me money, sister."

I turned to see a boy, his stomach bloated like a pregnant woman, his head like a large, wilting sunflower on a skinny stalk. I reached into my bag. I would have to be careful with my money, but how could I refuse a child?

I dropped a paisa into his open palm, noticing with shock that his forefinger was missing and his thumb was deformed.

My head reeled. I thought how lucky I was in spite of everything that had happened.

"Do you want your fortune read?" A gypsy woman was standing beside me in a skirt that showed her bare legs and ankles. Firm, round half-moons of breasts peeped boldly from beneath her blouse. I started. I had never seen a gypsy woman so close. She stood straight, bold, unashamed of her body. Her eyes were an unusually light brown: tawny and speckled with gold, like tigereye. She smiled.

"I don't have much money, sorry."

"I didn't ask for any," she pointed out.

I looked at her, puzzled.

"You look lost. What's a nice girl like you doing alone here?" She sounded concerned, not curious.

"I'm not lost. I'm looking for something," I replied.

"Ah. What is that something?" she asked.

"If you can tell my fortune, surely you can tell that?"

She smiled. "Perhaps you are looking for someone?"

I stared at her and then nodded slowly.

"Maybe I can help you find him," she said.

"Maybe." She was a stranger, but I wanted to trust her.

"You are looking for your brother," she guessed.

"Yes. Can you tell me where the nearest police station is and how to get there?" At a police station they would know where men went to enlist. Surely they would.

The gypsy nodded. "If you can walk, I can take you there."

She turned away from the main road into a tiny lane, striding ahead gracefully. We walked past mud huts with thatched roofs that looked as though they would be blown away in a monsoon. The roads smelled of human excrement. Children sat on doorsteps minding other children. I thought of the house I hated so much, how little I had thought about the world outside those walls, of all that I was sheltered from in the house in Madras and the grinding poverty at our doorstep.

Mangy stray dogs with patchy coats barked at me. I remembered how often I had brushed Raja's glossy fur.

Warnings crept into my mind, warnings about how gypsies were nothing but beggars and thieves. What if she snatched my money bag? I'd never find my way back through the maze of crisscrossing back alleys.

We turned and we were back on the bustling main road again. In front of us was a large red building—the Madras Municipal Court and the attached police station. I fished in my bag for the money and held out a few paisa.

She laughed, throwing back her head, revealing a row of startling, tobacco-stained teeth.

"I don't take money from children," she said. "May you find your brother. And may you return safely to your home."

She spat. A long red stain leaped across the black and white zebra stripes on the road.

Then she turned and was gone. I stared ahead at the forbidding front of the building.

The Officer

$\mathcal{I}$ took a deep breath. Appa had taught me during yoga lessons that the best way to calm nerves was to take long, deep breaths.

I squared my shoulders, adjusted my dusty half sari and walked up to the uniformed watchman.

"What do you want?" He was not friendly.

"I need to go in," I said.

"Why?" he asked dryly.

"I need to find out something."

"I asked you what you wanted." His voice assumed a threatening tone.

"I need to talk to the superintendent," I said, trying to sound confident.

He glared at me, as though to tell if I was joking. "Get out."

"Please, sir." I felt like a beggar now. "Please."

"Get out." He tightened his grip around his lathi menacingly.

A shiny black Hudson purred up to the gates. The watchman stepped back at once, touching his hand to his forehead in a smart salute. "Salaam, sahib!"

Desperate, I ran through the gates behind the car.

"Stop!" the watchman shouted, racing after me. "Stop!"

He caught the end of my braid and pulled. My head jerked back. I screamed with pain. Tears spurted into my eyes.

The window of the Hudson rolled down, and a radish red face called out in the crisp British accent I usually heard on the radio, "What's going on, Salim?"

"Just a beggar, sir," the watchman said. "An urchin."

"I'm not an urchin," I said hotly. "I'm not a beggar."

"Beggars don't speak English, Salim." The door opened and a long, slim body stepped out of the Hudson. The driver leaped out, his magnificent turban bobbing with confusion.

"What are you doing here, young lady?" The white man gave me a searching look.

My mind clouded with the image of white hands ripping apart a woman's blouse, an officer's lathi raining down on my father's bloody forehead. I forced the image out of my mind. "I need help, sir."

The steel gray eyes narrowed.

"My brother left home to enlist in the war effort without a good-bye. I want to see him."

"And you think I can help, do you?" he asked. His mouth was soft. "Tell me your story, young lady." His yellow hair looked wet. It was slicked back tidily under his thick khaki-colored hat. "You didn't come all this way to be silent, did you?"

It came tumbling out of me, all of it. Even the fact that my father had lost his mind in a protest march.

"So you came looking for your brother on your own, did you?" he asked.

I nodded.

"We could use you on our side, young lady," he said, smiling.

"I could never be on your side," I found myself saying, looking him levelly in the eye, wondering what he meant.

He laughed. "No, I suppose not. If I were in your position, which thankfully I am not, I would have said much the same thing."

"Can you help me, sir, or not?" I asked.

"Straight to the point, eh? Maybe I can help. Let's get you a cup of good strong Indian tea, shall we? Then we'll see if we can't find that brother of yours."

I followed him into his office hesitantly. Gilded fans whirred above my head, stirring the warm air.

"Sit down, sit down, plenty of chairs." He waved his hand at them and then reached behind him and pulled on a cord. A bearer appeared in a smart uniform with a pleated turban on his head.

"Two cups of chai, and would you grind some spices into it, please, Aarumugam." He pronounced the bearer's name perfectly. "Now, young lady, would you write your brother's name clearly, please? Age, date of birth and date he probably enlisted."

I did so, in my best handwriting. He picked up the telephone and dialed. He was talking to someone when the bearer returned, carrying a silver tray with two bone china cups of masala chai, cubes of white sugar and five Huntley and Palmer biscuits. The sweet, spicy milk tea warmed me.

When the officer finished his chai, he pushed the plate of biscuits closer to me, told me to "Tuck in," and then left me alone in the room for a while. I dug my toes into the jute mat on the floor and stared at the rows of leather-bound books on the shelf. I hadn't eaten anything since my two idlis, and spongy rice cakes didn't stay long in the stomach. It took a few hours, whatever it was he was doing. By the time he returned, I'd finished the biscuits and polished off the crumbs.

His eyes were twinkling. "I think we've found him, young lady. He should be at the army barracks near St. Thomas Mount. Do you know where that is?"

"No, sir."

"So what are we going to do if you don't know where the good saint's mountain is?"

"I can find it," I said.

"I've no doubt you can. I'll have my driver drop you off there," he offered.

"Thank you, but no, sir. I already have so much to thank you for."

"Beholden to the British, eh?" He chuckled.

I didn't know quite what to say.

"Tonight your brother might be boarding a train that will take him to a training camp in Delhi," he said. "Want to make certain you see him before he leaves, don't you?"

"Yes, thank you, sir."

"The pleasure is all mine, I assure you." He smiled.

"Once I get there, I can get back home on my own," I added.

He threw back his head and laughed. "Yes, yes, of course. Not turning my car and driver over to you for your use, you can be quite certain of that."

He shook his fountain pen slowly and began to write a letter with long, slanting strokes. He signed it with a flourish and sealed it. Then he pulled on the cord again. The bearer appeared and saluted.

"Escort this young lady to my car, would you, please? She needs to be driven to the army barracks at St. Thomas Mount. Tell the driver that, please. On my orders, in my car. Straightaway."

He turned to me again. "When you get there, young lady,

take this letter of introduction to the major, would you? It should ensure that you get a more decent reception than the one you had here."

"Thank you, sir."

"You've thanked me enough," he said, looking into my eyes steadily. "Run along now. And good luck."

St. Thomas Mount

The driver gazed at me, perplexed. The bearer repeated his instructions three times before the driver nodded me curtly into the Hudson.

I settled back into the soft seat. The car sped through the streets. In the distance, I saw a hill with a church on top of it, growing closer all the time.

The driver drove in through the gates of a large walled compound and stopped in front of a tall white building.

"I should go in?" I asked.

The driver nodded. I pushed open the door. The Hudson roared away, dust rising in its wake like brown smoke.

I stepped inside and walked up to the armed guard in the foyer. "I'm looking for the major. I need to give him this."

I showed him the letter. The freshly solidified red wax gave off a pleasant smell.

He made a move to take my letter.

"I have to deliver it to the major myself," I said.

He didn't question me any further. Instead, he escorted me

inside, stepping into an office for a few minutes to speak to the major before showing me in.

The major's gray eyes looked incongruous in skin that was no longer as light as it had once been—skin the color of pale brown beach sand. His neatly trimmed beard was covered with a net, the way amma used to cover her hair sometimes, those days long ago, when we had gone together to music concerts.

"I'm looking for my brother, sir," I said.

He twirled the tip of his mustache between his thumb and forefinger. I handed him the letter.

The major slid his large index finger under the envelope and broke the seal. He smiled as he read. A gentle smile.

"I see," he said at last.

He looked into my eyes like a benevolent grandfather. He was unlike anything I had imagined an army man would be.

He rang a bell. A uniformed soldier appeared. The major gave him instructions. "Your brother shouldn't be long. Would you like something to drink?"

I shook my head, but he had a bearer come in with a glass of water. I was sipping it when Kitta appeared.

I spluttered and choked. Kitta's hair had been shaven off. He was almost bald and dressed in the roughness of an army uniform.

"Go on, then, both of you," the major said, still smiling. "Get out of my office."

I had a sudden impulse to kiss the major's pale, wrinkled cheek. Instead, I thanked him quietly and followed my transformed brother out of the building.

When we were in the open air, we fell into pace with each other.

"What are you doing here, Vidya?" Kitta's voice was still the same under that strange uniform.

I stared at him, all that I'd wanted to say, every argument I'd prepared, forgotten.

He put his arm around my shoulders and steered me across the open parade ground. We sat down on a bench beneath the shade of a gnarled banyan tree.

"Come back, Kitta, please come back," I said.

"What, and get shot for being a deserter before I've been deployed?"

"Why can't you at least wait till you finish college?" I pleaded. By that time, perhaps the war would be over. Perhaps he could be delayed if not stopped.

"The Japanese have swept across Asia. I can't just wait and watch anymore." He sounded tired.

"One man more or less won't make a difference."

"So you think your brother won't make a difference? What a way to send your men off to war, telling them they don't count." He laughed. I was silent.

"I'm glad you came, Vidya," he said. "I wanted to see you again before I left."

"I thought I'd never hear from you again," I said. "You left without an address. Without anything."

"We didn't have a proper good-bye, did we?"

"I was so angry. Why did you tell Raman instead of me?"

"Because I knew you'd be angry," he answered. "I knew you wouldn't listen. Raman understands my opinion, even if he has a different one."

"I don't understand you."

He shook his head. "You just won't try to see my point of view, Vidya."

"I have, Kitta. I've thought about it ever since you left. But to me it's just wrong, killing people. Maybe you're right that Hitler and his lot are evil. But like Gandhiji says, the end doesn't justify the means, and I think war should never be a means to any end."

"It shouldn't, Vidya, but sometimes it is, can't you see that? We don't live in an ideal world."

I sighed. "I'm not going back to that prison of a house without you," I said.

"Hardly a prison, is it? You escape every evening through the pages of one book or another."

"I can't say what I want," I said. "I suffocate in silence."

"You gabble away in that journal Raman gave you."

"It's not enough," I said. "I'm going to leave. I'll beg or

something. I met a gypsy woman. She looked like she had freedom."

"Did she?" he asked. "She probably has less rice than periamma gives you to eat every day and kids with lice in their hair. Is that freedom for you?"

"I'll find a way to live on my own," I retorted. "I've saved up some money."

"Enough to live off all your life? I didn't realize my little sister was so wealthy. Maybe I should have asked you to buy us a new home instead of volunteering for the army."

I was forced to laugh. In spite of everything, he had found a way to make me laugh. He squeezed me tight.

"Don't be so angry about everything. Especially not with yourself," he said.

"What do you mean?" I asked. I couldn't help but notice that he seemed happier than he had in months, joking and smiling.

"You're angry with yourself about appa sometimes, aren't you? That's why you ignore him," he said.

"The person that's left behind isn't our appa," I said.

"No?"

"I don't think so," I said.

"I do," he said. "Anyway, it's not your fault. None of what happened. At all."

"How do you know?" I asked. "You weren't even there."

"I know."

"You don't, Kitta. I ran out of the car and joined some protestors. If I hadn't, appa would never have been beaten. He told me not to go and I didn't listen to him."

He heard my confession without any change of expression. "Something was bound to happen sooner or later, wasn't it?" he said. "He sacrificed his family when he joined the freedom struggle."

"Like you're doing now. You're sacrificing your family too."

"Maybe," he said.

"Men can march and protest and fight and shoot guns at each other and all we get to do is stay home and steam idlis," I said.

"And burn holes through the hearts of your fathers and brothers with those glaring eyes when you're angry. I should take you with me. Even Hitler would cringe if you stared at him long enough."

We laughed again, and I thought how much his voice sounded like appa's. "Remember when appa took us to see that film, Kitta? *Thyaga Bhoomi*?" I asked.

"About the woman who divorced her husband and went to join Gandhiji's nonviolent protests? Of course I do."

It was only the third time we'd ever been to a cinema. The British hadn't censored it because they didn't understand enough Tamil, appa had said.

"Remember how amma used to say, 'What if they catch cholera?' whenever appa bought us *cholam* on the beach?"

I could smell the roasting corn, covered in red chili powder, the vendor squeezing lime juice over the golden kernels.

"I wish he'd just died, Kitta." The whisper tore itself out of my throat before I could stifle it.

"I've wished that too," he admitted.

We sat in silence, and I imagined it, appa's death. Appa's stiff body flat on the floor, the relatives sitting around him in a circle, crying softly. The men carrying him to the cremation ground on a bamboo stretcher. A shroud covering his body. Kitta lighting the head of the funeral pyre. Flames leaping higher and higher behind my brother as he turned and walked away.

"Don't die, Kitta. Please don't die," I whispered.

"I'll do all I can to stay alive." He laughed, but I didn't join in.

"I'm scared they'll make me marry someone, Kitta," I said. "Without you, there'll be no one to stop them."

"You don't need me," he said. "Just sing off-key when the boy's parents come to look you over. Or fart in their faces when they make you parade in front of them."

"Yes, that's what I should start practicing. Farting on cue."

When our laughter faded into silence once again, he looked into my eyes more seriously than I had ever known he could be.

"Vidya, I'm frightened too. Frightened I'll be a coward. That I'll cry when they stick me on a battlefield."

I put my hand over his and squeezed hard. There was nothing left to say. We sat there together for a long time. The sun's rays had bled into the entire sky by the time he got up.

"You need to start soon so you'll get back before dark."

"Where will they send you, Kitta?"

"I'm not sure, but I'll write as soon as I can, I promise."

"I still think it's wrong, what you're doing."

"I know." He hugged me again. Tightly. Then he let me go and stepped backward, away from me. "Chin up now, Vidya, and get back safe."

"You get back safe too."

"I'll do my best," he said seriously. "Will you be okay?"

"I made it here all right, didn't I?" I said.

"You certainly did." He grinned and waved. "Jai Hind!"

I forced my features into a smile and waved. Then he ducked down and disappeared into one of the barracks.

I gazed for a while at the swinging roots of the banyan tree and thought of how we had played as children, hanging on to banyan roots and trying to push the other one off. How amma had always been worried we'd get hurt doing it. How appa had always let us play as long as we wanted.

I thought about the depth of appa's trust in nonviolence. His faith in his path had remained unshaken until the end. Had my brother inherited appa's self-confidence? Did Kitta believe in himself enough to survive the war he was joining?

I walked out of the compound and collapsed onto the pavement. It was dusty and caked with drying mud, but I didn't care. Dusk fell as tears came tumbling out of me for appa, for Kitta, for amma, for me, for the four of us, for the family that had perished forever. My sobbing was as ceaseless as the sound of the sea.

"Vidya?"

I looked up through the haze of my tears.

It was Raman.

The Return

"Come on. Let's find some other place to sit," he said.

I was too tired to resist. Raman pulled me gently, awkwardly to my feet and led me away, holding my hand.

We sat down at the bus stop on a low bench below a streetlamp. He sat close to me. I could feel his shoulder touching mine. I sagged against it and wept. He let the racked sobs shudder out of me until there were none left.

"Drink this." He forced a bottle of water to my lips.

I obeyed like a child.

"You look like you haven't eaten since you left."

"I'm not hungry," I said flatly.

"Can't help you there anyway. I didn't want to carry along a tiffin box. Did you meet Kitta?"

I nodded. We sat together in the darkness quietly for a long time. Then I asked, "How did you find me?"

"It's not that hard to trace the steps of a runaway girl who doesn't bother to cover them up," he said. "Your mother was worried when you didn't come home from school at the usual time this afternoon. She managed to let me and your grand-father know, and I left to look for you immediately. I suspected you'd gone to search for Kitta."

He paused. "Another part of me was frightened you'd just left. That I'd never see you again." He broke off, his voice suddenly hoarse.

I looked at the ground.

"You'll come home with me, won't you?" he whispered.

I nodded. I had nowhere else to go.

I followed him into a red bus, and he pulled me into the men's seats with him. I was too tired to see the shocked stares of the passengers. My head lolled against his shoulder and I slept until he woke me up and we had to get off.

We walked back, not touching, the rules of the house imposing themselves on us again.

Amma ran out of the house. She must have been waiting, watching for my return. She didn't wrap me in her arms until we were inside the compound wall. Then she wept, as though she would never stop.

I hated seeing her cry. After all that had happened to us, it was what I had done that made her break down in front of me. I hated myself for causing my mother's tears and I hated her for weeping because of me. A part of me wanted to shake her off and leave and pretend I hadn't seen her lose her self-control. But another part, a part I had not seen in a long time, made me stroke her graying hair until she stopped sobbing.

We entered the house together, the three of us.

"She's back!" periamma shouted. "That ungrateful girl."

Everyone came into the hall to see me. Even thatha left his study and descended the stairs. Periamma would have said more, but thatha surprised us all.

"Let the child eat and put her to bed," he said. "We can discuss this later."

His eyes met my tired gaze. I could not read his expression.

I heard his heavy footsteps climb back to his study and the sound of the rosewood door as it thudded shut.

The Proposal

The next morning I slept until amma shook me gently awake. Her face was tense and drawn.

"I've done your morning chores," she said. "It's nearly time for breakfast."

Periamma was muttering with her back to me as I walked into the kitchen. Her mounds of flesh were quivering with excited anger. "What shame that girl has brought on our family. What if Malati was still unmarried? It might have ruined my Malati's life!"

"Imagine if anyone ever heard of this," Sarasa chithi said, shuddering sympathetically.

"No one will," periamma said, suddenly directing her ferocity at Sarasa chithi. "You had better make sure that this story stays within the walls of this house, do you understand? I don't want your tongue wagging; I don't want the scandal following Malati as she settles down in her husband's home. I don't want her suffering because of this wretched girl's stupidity, dragging our name into the dust."

"Of course." Sarasa chithi sounded shocked. "I mean, of course not."

That was when they noticed my presence.

Periamma's voice went up by at least a few octaves. "Look at you! Look at you striding into the kitchen like a slut."

"Leave her on the street where she belongs, I said to my father, only he wouldn't listen," periappa yelled from the dining room. It was the first time I had heard a man join in the conversation of the women.

"Idiot father, idiot daughter," periamma said.

I stood in the doorway of the kitchen. I didn't care what they said now.

"Who will marry her now?" Sarasa chithi asked, loud enough for everyone to hear.

"There are a few families with idiot boys," periappa said loudly. "Surely we can find one of those."

I said nothing. My eyes searched for the man who had been my father. Had he missed me when I was gone?

Raman stood up. I looked at him in surprise. A mound of uneaten *uppuma* was still steaming on his plate.

"Have you had enough, Raman?" periappa asked solicitously.

"Yes, I've had enough."

"The cream of wheat is very sticky today. I suppose the women have been too shocked by Vidya's antics to pay attention to their cooking, poor souls," periappa said.

Laughter echoed through the kitchen and reverberated in the hall.

"I've heard enough about Vidya. Is that clear? Stop it," Raman's voice rang out.

There was a stunned silence. Periappa's mouth fell open, a half-chewed ball of uppuma still on his large round tongue.

"I'm going to marry her," Raman announced. "I asked your father for permission yesterday. So that's settled."

"What?" periappa said weakly. "What did you say, boy?"

"I'm marrying her," Raman repeated. "That's arranged. Last word."

Periappa began to babble. "Raman, my boy, don't be silly now. You have such a great future ahead of you, and what's all this nonsense? You are going to America next year and—"

I did not hear more. I dashed up to the library. It was as though something had caved inside of me, as though my mind had been shaken by an earthquake.

Within minutes, Raman entered, smiling widely.

I stared at him. I could not find words to express my emotions.

"We'll be married in two months' time, and in August, we'll sail to America. I thought you'd like it better than Britain, so I chose MIT over Oxford. I asked your grandfather yesterday. It's all arranged."

Hadn't I secretly wished for something like this to happen?

No, a voice said inside of me. Not like this. Not this way.

He waited. "Well, aren't you going to say anything?"

"I can't." My voice was thin, like a steel wire. "I can't think about it."

"Vidya?" He looked perplexed. "Vidya, are you feeling all right?"

"I need time," I said, my eyes filling with tears. "I need more time."

"For what?" He stared uncomprehendingly.

"Why didn't you ask me, if you really cared what I thought about America? Why didn't you tell me anything before?"

"I'd been thinking of it all along," he said softly. "But I meant for it to be a surprise. Then Kitta left, and I knew you needed someone to protect you. I had to do something right away."

"I want to do something with my life." My voice was trembling. "Something other than having babies."

"I thought you liked me," he said.

I couldn't deny that. So I didn't.

"I guess I went about it the wrong way," he said. "But come on! You know you want to marry me. I'll allow you to study. You know that."

I was silent.

"What do you want, Vidya? Some man who won't allow you to study and who'll lock you up behind the kitchen doors instead?"

Words finally formed on my tongue. "*Allow* me to study?" I hissed. "That's the problem, can't you see? Who are you to give me permission to study? Who are you to *let* me do what I want?"

He shuffled slightly. "I didn't realize," he mumbled.

"No, you didn't, did you? You'd act as though you owned me if I became your wife. You've started already."

"Perhaps you're right," he said. "I need to change. You could help me change."

"Not unless you treat me as an equal," I said.

"I would," he pleaded.

"Would you?"

"Yes," he said simply. "I would try."

I turned my face away from him to look at the wall. My cheeks were burning as though I had a fever.

He sat down on the window seat and massaged his temples with his hands. "I thought maybe you loved me."

"I thought I did too," I said, "until you just went and asked someone else about something so important. If I were your wife, would you consult me about major decisions or would you ask my grandfather's opinion? I don't think I really know who you are."

"I see," he said. His neck drooped like a wilting stem. He turned and shuffled out.

After he was gone from the room, I crumpled into the window seat. My eyes were too tired to focus. The room faded away. Outside the window, everything was a smoky blur.

He had failed me. He had asked thatha first.

The Diary

$\mathcal{I}$ sat in the library wondering what I'd done. I'd only meant to ask for more time. How did our conversation spiral so quickly out of control?

I opened the diary Raman had given me, and I shook my pen slowly to make the ink flow, and I tried to write.

My fingers trembled. I wrote his name again and again, Raman, Raman, Raman, Raman. Then I dropped the book on the window seat and slouched against the wall.

The door opened. I looked up hopefully.

But it wasn't Raman. It was periamma. She marched up to me and smiled, looking me up and down. I was about to turn my face away when she noticed my diary and pounced on it as a cat pounces on its prey.

"It's mine!" I shouted. "Give it back to me!"

She smiled with joy, toying with it, turning the pages with her pudgy fingers, sputtering with shock as she saw what I had written about her.

"Give it back!" I said.

She took it downstairs triumphantly. I followed her down, furious.

The men were just sitting down to lunch when she walked in, brandishing it as though it were a murder weapon that would finally set to rest a case that had spanned decades.

"Here!" she shouted. "Look at this, all of you. The girl has been reading and writing such vulgar things. Ungrateful, that's what her family is. First her brother spurns us and joins the army; now this girl turns away such a fine match. A prospect much too good for her, I'd say."

Raman sat in silence, looking at his feet. He did not rise to my defense. He did not say, "I gave her that diary." Though that would not have helped matters at all.

"Give it to me," periappa said presumptuously. "Let me see!"

But before he could grab it, thatha turned to me and said, "Is this really your book? Did you write it?"

"Yes," I said. "It is. But there's nothing vulgar in it. Only the truth. The truth of my thoughts."

"Then you won't mind if I read it," he said.

"It wasn't meant for anyone else," I said. "It was meant only for my own eyes."

"It has already been seen by others," he continued. "Perhaps it would be best if I read it too."

So I nodded and he took it.

Amma squeezed my hand tightly as I came into the kitchen. I went out again to serve the men their rice.

I paused in front of Raman's place. He stared at my feet and did not look at me. "Do you want any more rice?" I asked him softly, hoping he would look up.

He shook his head in response and said nothing. Not a word, not a look through the entire meal.

Before he got up to wash his hands, I stepped out of the kitchen, where Sarasa chithi and periamma sat with their heads touching, chattering like excited crickets.

"Where are you going?" periamma shouted, and then laughed harshly at something Sarasa chithi said in reply.

"Raman," I called softly. He walked past me as though I wasn't there.

I sat in front of my food, unable to swallow any of it. Amma stroked my hand silently.

That evening at dinner, I did my best to give Raman a chance to talk to me. I lingered by him every time I walked past. But he didn't raise his eyes even an inch off the floor.

I thought about it until my head hurt and I heard another voice within me. Telling me that I had been a fool. The greatest fool that ever lived. Living in a fairy-tale world but failing to see my prince when he tried to rescue me.

In Thatha's Study

The next morning after breakfast, thatha beckoned me. I climbed the stairs behind him and entered the holy sanctum of his study.

Above his writing desk hung a huge, prominent portrait of a woman that was decorated with a garland of roses, so fresh that their perfume permeated the still air of thatha's study. I stared at it. It was like looking into a mirror, a mirror of the future that reflected the way my face would look in another ten years.

Thatha smiled. "Yes," he said. "You look astonishingly like your grandmother. You seem to have inherited her spirit too."

"And temper?" I could not help asking.

He chuckled. "She controlled it much better than you do. Though perhaps you will learn to check it too, in time."

I stared at my grandmother's portrait.

"I'm sorry," thatha said. "You are right—that book was meant for your eyes only."

"It—It doesn't matter," I stammered. I hadn't thought patriarchs were capable of apologizing.

"You write well," he said. "Very well, in fact. Tell me, as you don't want to marry yet, what would you do if you were given more time?"

"Go to college."

"What would you do in college?" he asked.

"Study. Acquire knowledge."

"Why do you want all that knowledge?"

"The Vedas say that questioning is one of the ways to reach God," I replied.

"And what would you do with your questions and your knowledge before you reach God?"

"I would pass it on to others, as we are meant to," I said. "Other women. Other young women who want to study."

Thatha smiled. "In doing so, you would fulfill your Brahmin dharma, your traditional duty, would you not?"

"We possess too much wealth to call ourselves Brahmin," I said, remembering all I had read in the library and what appa had said when he was still with us. "We are not wise enough either. Besides, caste was never meant to be inherited. It has degenerated into a cruel custom that has nothing to do with the core of Hindu spirituality."

Thatha smiled again. "You argue like a scholar already. You will surely never marry any man. You will chase them all away."

I did not know how to react.

"So what will you do if we use some of your dowry to send you to study?" he asked.

"Do I have a dowry?" I asked.

He chuckled. "I have grown old. I am as easy to manipulate as a lump of wet clay. I haven't even thought about it for a day, and yet I am willing to say—to give you my word—that you may go to college."

I looked at him uncertainly. "You will let me go to college?"

He smiled. "Yes."

"Whatever happens?" I asked, still afraid to trust what he had said.

"I promise."

I began to smile. I wanted to throw my arms about his thin shoulders, but his heart would probably have stopped if I'd attempted such a public display of affection.

I smiled and smiled, searching for something to say. Before I found it, thatha asked, "What will you study, Vidya?"

I tried to focus enough to answer that question. I had never really given it much thought. Appa had barely mentioned college before the seeming reality had been snatched out of my hands and turned into a mocking dream.

Thatha's eyes twinkled. "Maybe you just want a bigger library?"

"As long as it's in a college," I said.

He laughed.

I knew I wanted to learn more. Learn enough to earn money to look after myself. And maybe to take amma and the man who was once my father out of this house into a home. My own.

My mind clouded again with the image of the woman my father had saved. Of his crumpled body lying on the stretcher. Of the doctors around him, trying to help.

Then the answer came to me, with such clarity that I was shocked I had not known it all along.

"I want to be a doctor." My voice was self-assured. I straightened my back. I felt confidence surge through me, giving weight to my joy, making it real.

"A doctor like your father," thatha mused.

"Yes," I said. "Yes, a doctor like my father." I remembered Kitta telling me appa would never be well again. Maybe he was right. But even so, I could help people the way appa had done. I would cure others, if not appa himself. I would save lives.

"Your father would be proud of you," thatha said.

"He would be proud of both his children." It slipped out of me before I could check myself. Thatha did not react. I couldn't tell if he had really not heard or if he was pretending. At least he didn't yell at me for bringing up Kitta.

"Thatha," I said, still struggling to thank him. "You don't know how much this means to me."

"Go downstairs," he said at once, shooing me away. "Go and tell your mother." He looked uncomfortable but pleased all the same.

We smiled at each other. At the door, I turned to thank him again, but before I could, he waved his hand and said, "You'll thank me best by studying well at college." I nodded. "Shut the door behind you, Vidya."

Amma was waiting at the foot of the stairs. I felt as if I was floating down toward her. I saw her eyes brighten and the anxiety drain from her face.

"You had a good talk with thatha?" she asked.

I hugged her. "Better than good," I said. "Much, much better than good. The best talk!"

I thought how glad appa would have been to know I was finally going to college.

"Amma," I said to her. "I need to tell you and appa something. Something good."

Her eyes began to well up with tears and she wiped them away with the pallu of her sari.

We joined appa in the main hall. Amma held one of his hands and I held the other. His grasp was like a child's— clinging.

"College, appa," I said. "I'm going to college to be a doctor so I can help you."

I thought I saw appa's eyes glimmer. Something seemed to

move within the shell that was appa, where at least a fragment of his soul still surely survived. And I know I felt his hand squeeze mine gently, as he used to do when he was pleased with me.

A bit of appa was hidden somewhere within that body. And he was alive in amma, and in me, and in Kitta too, wherever Kitta was now.

"Vidya," amma said. "I'm so happy for you."

Then I knew I had to tell her what had happened the day of the protest march.

"Amma," I said. "You need to know what happened the day appa was injured."

Her face sobered. "Vidya," she said gently, "if you're sure you want to talk about it, I'm here to listen."

"I want to," I said. "After we dropped periappa off at the station that day, a mob flooded the street we were on. We had to stop driving. Appa told me to stay near the car. But I didn't. I ran away from him. I ran into the crowd. And then." I took a deep breath. "And then the policemen came and started beating everyone. There was a woman." I stopped. I could see her face, her hand holding the Indian flag high up above her head.

"You don't have to talk about it if you don't want to," amma whispered.

I took another deep breath, closed my eyes, and told her

every detail of what had happened that morning. "So it was my fault that appa was beaten," I finished.

"Is that what you've been thinking all this time?" amma asked. "That all this is your fault?"

I nodded and looked away.

"Look at me," amma said, gently turning my face toward hers. "What happened would have happened anyway. One day or another. It had nothing to do with you. It would have happened even if you had been inside the car. Appa would have seen something, and he would have tried to stop it." She paused. "It is not your fault." She repeated it again, with a pause between each word. "You must never think that again."

She reached for my hand and pressed it, and warmth flowed from her fingertips into mine. A great weight seemed to lift itself off me, as though a stone that had been weighing down my heart had finally rolled away.

But later that night, I felt a hunger that had nothing to do with food. Inside me was an emptiness that cried out for Raman, an emptiness that even the promise of college could not fill.

The Evacuation

The next day at breakfast, I was too tired to try speaking to Raman again. I tried to concentrate on college, nothing but college.

Before the men left the meal, thatha beckoned.

"We have been notified that your school has closed, Vidya," he said.

I stared at him in confusion. "Closed?"

"The British have ordered an evacuation. Anyone in Madras city who can leave must leave."

"Why?" I asked.

"The Japanese are coming closer," thatha replied. "The British fear that they will take over the Bay of Bengal and the Indian Ocean and begin to bomb our harbor cities."

"Where will we go?" I asked.

"The men will stay behind," thatha said. "The children and the women will leave. Your aunts will go to their parents' homes. And you and your mother will pack up your things today and leave with your father on the night train to Coimbatore tomorrow evening. One of the men of the house will accompany you on your journey."

"Coimbatore?" I repeated. I shook my head confusedly.

"Your mother's brother, Bala maama, lives there," thatha said. "I sent him a telegram to ask that he look after the three of you until it is safe to return to Madras again. He has agreed."

"What about school?" I asked.

Thatha smiled. "I knew you would ask that. You can finish fifth form in Coimbatore this year. By next year, this nonsense will probably be over, and you can finish your final year of school here, in Madras."

I wondered where we would be in a year. If Kitta was right, the Japanese might have taken over by then.

"Don't look so worried," thatha said. "I have given you my word about college, and I haven't forgotten. If Madras is still evacuated next year, I will send you to a college somewhere else."

I smiled at him gratefully before I realized that thatha had said the men would be staying behind—though we would take appa with us. If I left tomorrow night, I might never see Raman again. He would probably leave for America in a few months, while I was in Coimbatore.

As I helped amma pack, my mind swirled with images of the tall *peepal* trees in front of the great brick building of a medical college. Of the stone benches on which the students sat, of the long road that lay outside its whitewashed compound wall and silver sheet of afternoon sea that swept past it, beyond the strip of sandy beach.

And then my thoughts filled with images of gardens and of a girl who had once climbed fruit trees with her brother—of the past that was irrecoverable and of the daughter I would never have—the future with Raman that I had flung away.

Had I done the right thing in refusing him?

My head said yes, but my heart said no.

I could not promise to be his wife. But I could not see life without him. How had I hurt him so much, he who had been such a good friend to me? And yet if he had really loved me, how could his caring end so abruptly? I could hardly believe that I had served him dinner last night and breakfast this morning without his once looking into my eyes.

That evening before dinner, I ran upstairs to the library, hoping Raman would be there. He wouldn't let me leave without at least trying to say good-bye. I sat waiting, the diary he had given to me on my lap, the grandfather clock ticking away the time. He did not come.

When the clock struck half past seven, I put the diary away. I was not going to let him leave without a word. I would enter the men's hall if I had to.

As I shut the library door behind me and turned down the narrow corridor, I heard footsteps. I rushed down the corridor and nearly ran into Raman.

"Raman, I needed to speak to you before we left," I said.

"I was coming to talk to you," he said.

"Raman, I'm sorry," I said. "I'm really sorry."

"You shouldn't be," he said. "You taught me a lot. You made me see things about me that I need to change."

"I've learned a lot from you too," I said. "I can't imagine how I'll bear life in this house next year with you and Kitta gone."

"You'll think of college, and that goal will keep you going," he said.

"I'll think of you too," I said earnestly.

His eyes flickered for a second, but he didn't say anything other than "Good luck."

"Good luck to you too. I'll keep you in my prayers," I said.

He nodded briefly and turned. His footsteps receded from me.

"Raman!" I called.

He looked back questioningly.

"I just need more time. That's all I asked for. More time."

His face was a mask that I could not read.

"I can't promise to be your wife, not yet. But I can promise to write. I can write you letters, can't I?"

"No," he said uncertainly. "You won't write. You just want freedom from me and everything else."

"I will," I insisted. "Writing is what I do best. I can promise that much. I *do* promise that much."

"Don't make promises you can't keep."

"I can keep this promise, Raman. Help me. Please. I'm frightened to promise more."

"What are you scared of?" he asked.

"I've lost so much, Raman. And now, finally, I've found freedom."

He looked into my eyes a long time. His gaze washed away the walls I had so carefully erected around my feelings. He must have felt it. And then he smiled. It was a long time since I had seen his smile.

"I'll write and write and write," I said. "Every single day that you are away."

"Don't make promises you can't keep," he repeated.

"I can keep my word," I said earnestly. "I know I can. Will you reply?"

"What do you think?" he said.

"Raman, one day it will be more than letters. I know it. One day we'll be together again, and then I'll talk so much you'll want me to shut up. And I'll let our daughter run around in the sun and climb trees like a monkey. And you'll regret you ever married me."

It slipped out of me too late for me to stop myself. It was then that I realized I truly loved him, even if it would be years before I could bring myself to say those words that he wanted to hear.

Raman's smile was wider than ever, and his eyes were no longer just twinkling—they were dancing. But when he spoke, he didn't point out that I had actually used the word *married*. "I'll wait for my Vidya's letters. Between one letter and the next, I'll try to live an interesting life so I can write to you about it."

"It doesn't matter what you tell me," I said earnestly. "I won't find your letters boring. I'll read every word, I promise."

"That's a lot of promises you've made me today. I wish the British had evacuated Madras earlier."

I laughed.

Raman wrote down the address of the college he'd be studying at. MIT, in Boston, Massachusetts. We looked up Boston in the atlas. It was on the East Coast of America. It was, he said, where the American colonists had thrown tea into the harbor to protest British taxes. Like Gandhiji marching to Dhandi to make salt in protest of British law.

The next evening, amma, appa and I stood together in the great hall, ready to take our leave. Thatha came down, smiling, Raman beside him.

"Raman's family lives in Coimbatore," thatha said to me as I stared at them, slightly bewildered. "So he has agreed to accompany you and your mother there and see that you are safely dropped off at your uncle's home. He may as well leave Madras, at least for a while, given the evacuation order. And we couldn't send you and your mother alone without a male escort."

Raman and I looked at each other. Amma smiled, and thatha nodded at us approvingly. I saw then that Raman had spoken to thatha again to let him know that we had agreed to be married, that we would correspond with each other, to obtain thatha's permission for this liberty.

This time, I wasn't angry that Raman had spoken to thatha. I was glad.

Letters were the bridge I would build for myself to walk

across, a bridge I would cross slowly. And Raman would be there for me on the other side, waiting.

And even in the midst of all the uncertainty and change that lay ahead, of the reality of the evacuation and the Axis creeping closer to Indian soil, and of Kitta fighting on some faraway battlefield, I felt nothing but pure joy for a few moments: joy that I would soon be leaving the house, joy that I would go to college and that someday Raman and I would be more than friends.

Thatha walked to the verandah to see us off. Periamma, periappa, Sarasa chithi and her husband followed without much enthusiasm. I bowed to them as they stood in a long line. I said the traditional good-bye, "I leave now, but I will return."

They quickly repeated, "Leave, but come back," saying the second half of the traditional greeting so softly I hardly heard it. I smiled, but none of them smiled back. They returned indoors quickly with periamma muttering, "Good riddance," under her breath.

Thatha accompanied us all the way to the gate. Raman carried the two heaviest suitcases, and I carried the lightest one. Amma held appa by the hand.

I wondered if I would ever see thatha again, if this was our last good-bye, if the Japanese would bomb Madras into oblivion. I turned when we reached the end of the street. Thatha was still standing at the gate, watching us. He raised his hand in a final gesture of blessing and farewell, and I choked up. But by the time we were at the station, excitement about the future had driven my worries away like a breeze blowing away a cobweb.

I couldn't sleep on the train that night. Raman was shy to speak to me in front of amma, so he didn't say much, but he smiled a lot. I lay awake on my hard wooden berth, looking at the tiny purple-blue night-light on the ceiling of the compartment as the train thudded rhythmically on the rails, excited for the first time by the thought of college and marriage and of the two worlds that were both miraculously within my grasp.

The next morning, as the train pulled into the station, I saw Bala maama waiting to receive us, his face beaming with welcome. And before the train stopped moving and the four of us stepped onto the platform, I had a feeling of coming home.

Madras, August 14, 1942

My Dearest Raman,

I am sitting in the library, watching the sky blur from pink to charcoal gray, remembering the many hours we spent together here. I miss you already, though it was just this morning that you left on the first leg of your journey to the United States. Periamma probably wants me downstairs, working on something or another, but she no longer has as much power over me as she once did. I suppose it's because we're engaged now and because I'm going to college. Returning to the house yesterday, I felt years older—no longer the child who had left Madras just a few months ago.

I am glad we had a chance to live with Bala maama and his family over the summer—what a strange summer it was, harrowing and yet so full of hope. I am not sure how amma or I would have got through it at all except for the support from Bala maama's family—their affection, their joy in my good fortune, their kindness toward appa.

And it was fun to play with Raja again—I am so glad he likes their home.

Most important, of course, was your support your letters and all those visits you made to Coimbatore to see me and your family. I confess I was frightened of how they would react to the news of our engagement. What a relief it was to see that your parents and siblings were so completely happy for us!

I think of you turning back to wave to me at the end of the lane this morning, dressed in your shiny shoes and your new suit, ready to cross the seas in a time of war, and I worry about your safety—but only a little. Somehow, I am convinced that you will reach those distant shores safely and that the country you sail to is the country that will help us win this interminable war.

It is Kitta's life that seems to hang in the balance, and I often fear that I will never see him again. After you left this evening, thatha gave me and amma a packet of letters that Kitta had written. I don't know why thatha didn't forward the letters to Coimbatore—but I cannot tell you how happy I felt to see that packet, to know that thatha had saved the letters for us. Surely thatha cannot mean what he said about Kitta being dead to him? Perhaps thatha will never forgive my brother entirely, but amma says that not destroying the letters is a first step toward some kind of reconciliation.

Kitta writes guardedly, carefully, and I cannot hear his voice in his words. I know all our letters are monitored by censors now, but I fear there's another reason why Kitta's lines sound so strange. I fear that he is starting to see the awful truth of the path he has chosen—and though he has the courage and determination to see it through, it cannot be easy for him to train to use weapons to kill, to curb his questioning mind and always follow a white man's orders.

Kitta foresaw many things. The Japanese did capture the Andaman Islands and set foot on Indian soil, they dropped a few bombs on Madras, and some enemy ships and submarines hovered off the coast like threatening clouds, but somehow the tide of war seems to be changing and keeping them at bay. So perhaps Kitta is right and violence is the fastest way to win this war, but can it really be the only alternative? I hear my heart scream that it cannot be—that violence is merely a reaction, never a real answer.

I wonder too what will happen when we are a free nation because we will be, one day. After the oppression of foreign conquest is gone, will we still have the courage to continue on the path of nonviolence, to strive for the higher ideals that Gandhiji speaks of, for Tagore's heaven of freedom "where the world has not been broken into fragments by narrow domestic walls"?

My head spins so much when I think of all that, I must stop. For the rest of this final school year, I will have to do what I somehow managed to do those terrifying months we spent in Coimbatore when the Japanese flew their bombers across some of our cities—force myself to concentrate on my schoolbooks and do well in my final exams. So I can go to college, so I can make our dreams of the future come true.

Today I wrote the last entry in my diary—the gift you gave me long ago. Its pages are full now, as though it knows I will not need it anymore. Today and tomorrow and the day after, I will have to write letters—to Bala maama and his family, who treated us so well during the long hot summer in Coimbatore, and to my old friend Rifka, and to you, of course. I smile when I think how far those bits of paper will travel—from India all the way across the globe to a land that has much in common with ours. A colony that broke the British yoke as we will one day. A place to which persecuted people flee now as they once did to the shores of our country.

A nation that is also different from India. Young. Pulsing with potential. Different from us in ways I can only imagine, ways that you will write to me about before I can discover them myself.

A nation dedicated to the idea of freedom, the ideal for which we are fighting, all the way across the Atlantic and

Madras, August 14, 1942

*half of the Asian continent. A nation with the promise of
liberty and justice for all.*

A nation I will one day visit to join you.

Until then I remain,

Your loving friend,

Vidya

Author's Note

While the world was undergoing one of the most violent episodes in history, India experienced a new type of revolution: a nonviolent freedom struggle. The unique movement initiated by Gandhiji (better known in the West as Mahatma Gandhi) was sustained by the sacrifices of countless Indians who had the extraordinary courage to fight without compromising their belief in compassion. I am proud to count my father among those who played their part in the battle for India's freedom.

Perhaps because of its role in the world's first nationwide nonviolent movement, India's involvement in World War II is often overlooked. The British Army used resources from many colonies, including India, to fight the war, and so many Indians enlisted in the ranks that the British Indian contingent became the largest all-volunteer force to participate. There are a number of memorials to World War II veterans, but few of these acknowledge the contribution of soldiers from non-Western nations.

A few members of my extended family participated in the war effort. One of them, Shri Cuddalore Padmanabhan Aiyar, who enlisted in the navy, was forced to walk all the way from Burma (now known as Myanmar) to India after the fall of Rangoon, through forests filled with Japanese soldiers. As a child, I often wondered why he, the only son in a traditional Brahmin household, had decided to take up such an unorthodox position. Kitta's character was born out of that question.

In writing *Climbing the Stairs,* I also drew on a number of real events. Madras (now called Chennai) was evacuated in the spring of 1942. The scars left by a bomb dropped by the Japanese on a British fort in the city are still visible today. There were reports that a German submarine was sighted off the Madras coast, and the Japanese occupied the Andaman and Nicobar Islands of India for a few years. However, the Axis powers did not mount a sustained campaign directly against the Indian mainland, and bombing was sparse. My mother and her brother S. Ramachandran, who experienced the evacuation of Madras, remember air-raid drills, war reports on the radio and the fearful threat of Japanese invasion. During this tumultuous time, they lived in an extended family household, similar to that described in the novel. Later, my uncle chose to pursue a graduate career at MIT, just as Raman does in the novel, rather than study in England (which, at the time, was a more common choice for Indian men).

Vidya's personality is very much her own, but her story undoubtedly owes something to the few women I knew who grew up in the 1940s and were successful in their searches for personal expression, most of all my mother. As an adolescent, my mother spent her evenings in the large upstairs library of the extended family home, reading while minding her baby sister. She became a lawyer, the chief editor of two legal journals and the author of numerous legal texts. In this, she was encouraged and supported my paternal grandfather, Shri A. N. Aiyar, one of India's most brilliant legal minds. He provided the inspiration for thatha's role in the novel. His groundbreaking commentaries were published in numerous gold-embossed tomes that lined the bookshelves of our home library—a wood-paneled room where I first discovered my love for the written word. Fortunately, I was never forbidden from climbing the stairs to enter it!